LION
OF THE
SKY

RITU HEMNANI

BALZER + BRAY
An Imprint of HarperCollins*Publishers*

Balzer + Bray is an imprint of HarperCollins Publishers.

Lion of the Sky
Copyright © 2024 by Ritu Hemnani
All rights reserved. Printed in the United States of America.
No part of this book may be used or reproduced in any manner
whatsoever without written permission except in the case of
brief quotations embodied in critical articles and reviews. For
information address HarperCollins Children's Books, a division of
HarperCollins Publishers, 195 Broadway, New York, NY 10007.
www.harpercollinschildrens.com

Library of Congress Control Number: 2023943316
ISBN 978-0-06-328448-7

Typography by Celeste Knudsen
24 25 26 27 28 LBC 5 4 3 2 1
First Edition

For my three colors of hope,
Anoushka, Nadia, and Tarun,
and for my sky, my endless horizon,
Sunil

PART I: LIFTING OFF

DON'T LET GO

My kite comes to life
in the endless blue,
free and wild
as it
fights
     and
          snaps,
bucks   and   whips.

Hold on tight, Raj,
says my grandfather, Nana.
Soon the wind
will change in your favor,
just as long as you
don't let go.

It pulls in the wind
that roars and bites.

I wait before I pitch my kite,
sending it soaring high
above the mango trees,
like a rocket to the sky,
before its nose
ducks in a dolphin dive
that curls to a glide
alongside the Kirthar hills,
          its tail flickering, a chasing serpent
               sailing above the sparkling Indus.
                    With a spectacular finish of twists,
                         it spins like a pinwheel
                              in the blustery breeze.

DARING

I fly
through the fields of Sindh,
of wildflowers and birdsong,
my suthan pants flapping,
cool wind against my cheeks.

As my heart soars
high with my kite,
I dare to hope I just might
win the Kite Festival

for everyone to see.

EMPTY HAND

Then I trip,
with a bruised chin,
grazed knee,
and an open, empty hand.

A hand with
rapped knuckles
from Masterji's wooden stick,
reminding me
of all the math tests
I've failed at school
and all the
fractions
   angles and
      equations
that never add up
to an answer I can understand.

As my kite tumbles away
I sit, staring at
the backs of my hands.

My body stings
and now I'm not sure
I can win the Kite Festival,
not sure I want everyone
I know to see,

especially Baba.

JUST MAKE SURE

Ready to try again, Raj?

Nana has fetched
my crumpled kite,
hands it to me
with a smile that makes
the wrinkles on his face
fly wide,
while the wind
ruffles my hair
like his fingers,
and the sun heats my back
like his warm embrace.

I shake my head.

> *What's the point, Nana?*
> *I'll only fall again.*

Nana's gentle eyes sparkle.

Fall seven times
if you must, he says.

Just make sure
you stand up eight.

GUIDE

Nana gives me
his hand
and I hold on tight
as he pulls me up.

Soon my kite and I
are climbing
through the sky
    like a bird gliding,
    like a diamond shining
        under a sky
        of invisible stars,
            the wind just like Nana,
            helping me fly
                and guiding
                me home.

CROWN

There's a buzz
around Sindh
with everybody
talking
    shopping
        working
to prepare
for India's Independence Day
on August 15, 1947.

Baba hurries to make
sherwani suits
to sell in his garment store
for all the big, important leaders
of our newly freed land.

My brother Vijay,
who is seventeen
and good with numbers,
helps Baba
measure, cut, stitch,
and even balance his accounts.

Baby sister, Maya,
who is nine
and also good with numbers,
helps Amma
measure, stir, bake,
and even fry dishes for the celebration.

That leaves me—
Raj, aged twelve,

invisible, with a big appetite,
and scared of almost everything,
especially numbers.

But Amma named me Raj
because it means king.

*One day you'll be the king
of something,* Amma told me.

Now with the Kite Festival
coming,
I'm ready to claim
my crown.

IQBAL

Iqbal and I weren't always friends.
Not till I was eight
and got stuck high up
a mango tree.

He's Muslim, after all,
and wears his crisp white topi.

And I'm Hindu, after all,
and wear my dark red ajrak cap.

There I was,
too scared to jump down or climb higher.
Iqbal scratched his head, had a laugh,
then clambered up,
branch after branch
past me.

To lend a hand?
A word of support?

No!
He peeled three golden mangoes,
one
        by
                one,
sank his teeth into their plump flesh,
letting sweet juice dribble
down his chin.

I was envy green
with itchy feet,

but no matter how I tried,
I couldn't reach him.

I was too afraid
until he threw mango seeds
at my head,
one
        by
                one,
and that taught me
very quickly
how to fly up and down
a mango tree.

MIRROR

Safe on the ground
Iqbal and I
stared at each other
as if we were looking in a mirror.

He was fair and trim
with a mole next to his lip.
I was dark and plump
with a scar above my eye,
but we were exactly
the same height.

His kameez
was long and green,
crumpled and stained,
and his shalwar pants
kissed the top of his champals.

My kurta shirt
was loose and blue,
clean and pressed,
with a fitted collar and buttons,
and my suthan pants
sat snug above my juttas.

He prayed to Allah
and didn't eat pork.

I prayed to many gods
and didn't eat beef.

He said,
I know how to arch my neck
and spit
far as that mango tree.

> I said,
> *I don't believe you!*

He said,
I do!
I'll teach you how
if you promise
to always be my friend.

NO BETTER FRIEND

Iqbal taught me many things
after that.

How to blow bubbles with my spit,
how to cross my eyes,
how to dive deep into the Indus
and catch a slippery,
floundering prize.

How to pick the ripest mango,
which he always saved for me
in exchange for the softest chikoo,
the tender flesh
melting in our mouths.

The one thing I taught Iqbal
was how to fly.

As a gift for his ninth birthday
Amma helped me choose
the saffron-and-green patang
from the market.

When Iqbal saw it he cried
and said there wasn't a better kite,
or friend,
in the whole world.

One day I will fly
across the sky like this kite
to see faraway lands,
Iqbal said, the first time
his kite took off in the wind.

But you'll bring back
treats filled with
salt and sweet, right?

Forever thinking
about your stomach, Raj!
Yes, I might travel the world,
but I'll always come home.

And home is where I'll be.

KING OF KITES

The Kite Festival
will have two winners.

The King of Kites award for the flyer
with the best tricks
and the Kite Fighter award
for the flyer who cuts down
the most kites.

Though it might be easier for some
to use a manjha,
the kite string coated with powdered glass,
to cut the inside of another kite

like Baba used to
like Vijay used to

I know I want to win
not by cutting down kites
but by the skill of my tricks

so my kite stays light,
      twirls and flips
            lifts and dips
                  to knight me
                        the King of Kites.

TAMIR

Tamir is Iqbal's broad-built
sixteen-year-old cousin
with a hairy chin
who searches for trouble
as if it were buried treasure.

He waits at the school gate
slapping heads, tripping feet,
pinching coins from boys and girls
just for fun.

Come back here! Tamir shouts
after a boy who dares to run.

The boy shoots past us
and hurries down a lane
to the right.

Which way? Tamir booms,
charging toward us.

> *Left! He went left!* Iqbal shouts.

Thanks, cousin! Tamir calls.

> *Come on,* whispers Iqbal,
> pulling at my kurta sleeve.
> *Let's get out of here*
> *before he finds out I lied.*

PUNISHMENT

Masterji calls my name.

Slowly I stand,
searching his wall
of past star students,
and find Vijay's face smiling back.

Masterji's stick lifts high
and my eyes squeeze tight,
hands trembling
as his sharp, swift *thwack*
leaves my knuckles
cracked and raw,
the same color as the big
fat zero on my paper.

Then, even worse, his smirk
means I need to squat
and rise up
like a clown
up and down before the class,
who laugh
until Iqbal takes out
his slingshot and handful of rocks,
and
one
        by
                one
their mouths lock.

I raise my chin as I squat,
feeling smug that

Masterji's punishments
have failed
to make me cry.

Then I realize why
he's still wearing that
sly sneer.

Standing at the door
with a face flushed
with shame
is Baba.

DISGRACE

Masterji complains
that I am lazy and distracted,
not at all like
my hardworking,
high-achieving brother,
who beams down at all of us
from Masterji's wall.

That he has no choice
but to give me an F.

Baba's eyebrows lower,
his face twists in disgrace.

He folds his hands
to prostrate,
asks for one more chance,
saying he himself
will help me.

It feels good
to have Baba speak on my behalf,
but his look of disappointment
that I'm
not like him
            not good at math
                    not good enough
                    to help our family business

hurts far worse
than all Masterji's punishments
put together.

FREEDOM

My favorite time of day
is when my kite releases into the wind.
It soars above the earth
with Iqbal's,
not higher, not lower,
but side by side, like the two of us.

So high above the ground
they fly,
free like
I'm feeling now,
where math numbers
don't exist
and Masterji's stick
and words
can't hurt me.

You're the King of Kites, Raj!
shouts Iqbal.

I feel free like India
soon will be.
Free as a bird with its cage door open
with the British troops leaving
with independence coming
and our own leaders,
        and our own flag,
                and our own song.

Our carefree kites
dip, dive, and dance above
and it looks like freedom.

CHILI POWDER

Amma rises early
to bathe and pray,
her gold bangles jangling,
till she catches me
in the kitchen again.

Raj?

> *I was hungry and couldn't wait,*
> *I say, swallowing a spoonful of dal.*
> *It's delicious, but I thought*
> *it might taste better with . . .*

Amma gasps when she sees
I've added a teaspoon
of red chili powder to the dal.

Raj! How many times
have I told you not to—

> *Mukhe maaf kajo, Amma!*

We sit down
to a breakfast of dal pakwan,
the creamy-flavored lentils,
spicy mint coriander chutney,
and deep-fried crispy sweetbread
mingling in my mouth
before I swallow with relish.

Neha, the dal
is especially good today,
says Baba, taking another
spoonful.

When he isn't looking,
Amma and I
exchange a smile.

TUMMY PAIN

Baba and Vijay
are excited today.
General Chelmsford will visit
our store to collect the new suit
that Baba agreed
to let Vijay make.

If he's happy with it,
he'll order twelve more!
Vijay says, his eyes shining.

Baba has a woody scent
of Godrej soap
and is wearing his
gold chain, gold ring,
and the watch
his father left him.

The brown leather strap
is old and worn,
but the timepiece is perfect
in cogs, gold, and glass
and only comes out
on special occasions.

       It will bring us luck today,
       he says.

              I will bring you luck!
              says Maya, jumping
              on Baba's knee,
              as her arms wrap around

his neck, and she pecks
his cheek.

That you will!
he says, kissing her forehead.

Maya slurps up her milk,
then complains of tummy pain,
so Baba lets her play
with his father's watch.

I've never been more envious
of tummy pain.

SWALLOW

Baba pours his chai
from cup to saucer,
raising it carefully to his lips
and slurping loudly,
as Amma and the house girls
scurry around him
with his lemon-water finger bowl,
freshly pressed jacket,
and lunch tiffin of
spinach and vegetable curry
with steaming-hot phulko.

I am shifting in my seat.

In my head
I proudly announce
that I am planning to win
the Independence Day
Kite Festival.

Baba pulls me onto his knee,
gives me a squeeze,
Vijay slaps my back, and
Maya covers me in lucky kisses
as Amma says,
I knew I named you Raj
for a reason.

But with the rush
and excitement of the day,
there's no time to share
what I want to say,

so along with breakfast,
I swallow my words
and keep them in my belly
for tomorrow.

BABA'S LUCKY WATCH

We've all heard the story
of how Baba's father, Dada, was more
than just a tailor.

*He had a special instinct for business,
as every Bhaiband Sindhi should,*
Baba says as he sits to tell us
the story again.

One day a Persian poet
came to Dada's store,
asking for a new shalwar, headdress,
and robe.

I have no money to pay you,
the poet said.

> *It is no matter,* said Dada.
> *Simply pay what you believe
> these garments are worth.*

The poet was so delighted
with his clothes
that he presented Dada
with a book of poems
he himself had written.

The book was put on display
for customers to see.
One week later, it caught the eye
of the commissioner of Sindh,
Robert Giles.

This poetry is exquisite!
Name your price for the book
and I will pay it.

Dada thought for a moment.

Kind sir, the value of this book
is more than what you can pay me
in rupees.

Then how shall I pay you?

With your most treasured possession.

Both pairs of eyes fell on the
commissioner's watch.

A circular white and brown dial
sat proudly on a square silver base
with brown leather straps
and Roman numerals for hour markers.

It was a gift from my parents
when I received my posting.
It's a Rolex Oyster—specially
crafted with a sealed case
to make it waterproof.
I couldn't possibly—

No matter, said Dada,
placing the poetry book
back on display.

Within ten minutes,
Commissioner Giles walked out
of Dada's store
with the poetry book in hand
and in Dada's palm lay
what was to become
his most treasured possession—

not because of what it was worth
but because of how he earned it.

KAJU MITHAI

A large pot of cashew nuts
bathed in sugar, water, milk, ghee,
and freshly ground cardamom seeds
bubbles on a low flame.

Amma rolls the dough
between layers of wax paper,
then adds a sheet of edible silver foil
and reaches for a sharp knife.

May I cut the kaju, mehrbani?
I ask, with pleading eyes.

> *I can cut kaju far better*
> *than Raj,* whines Maya.

> *We need perfect diamond shapes*
> *for General Chelmsford,*
> *so I will do the cutting today,*
> says Amma.

But I can do it, look,
I say, grabbing a knife
and slicing a deep, straight line so smooth
I can't help but smile.
But it's then, when I take
my eyes off the knife, that I slice
my finger too.

Blood oozes over the counter,
drips onto the floor,

but worse than the stinging
is Maya screaming
until Amma wraps my finger
in muslin
and presses tight.

WARNING

When Baba sees my finger,
his eyes grow soft
and he kisses the top of my head.

Then he places a hand
on my shoulder, looks me in the eye,
and tells me that men
were born to protect and provide.

We calculate and trade, Raj,
we do not clean or bake.

> *But Baba . . .*

He raises his hand to silence me.

See what happens
when you get involved
in things you aren't supposed to?
All it does is spill blood and cause pain.

Baba says he knows
I want to help
with General Chelmsford's
visit today,

But the best thing you can do
to help us all from now on
is stay out of the kitchen.

Though his words are gentle,
his eyes are firm.

RAG CLOTH

After school,
Amma, Maya, and I
rush to Baba's garment store
in the center of town,
with our basket filled with
diamond-shaped kaju mithai.

I inhale the scent
of cashew nuts and cardamom
and hope there will be some left over
after General Chelmsford
has his fill.

If he praises Vijay's suit
and orders twelve more,
we'll give him the whole basket,
warns Amma.

Before we can reach Baba's store,
we see a large gathering
on the street outside.

In the middle of the crowd
stands tall and barrel-chested
General Chelmsford,
with three officers behind him.
His arms are flailing
as his red mustache
huffs left and right.

> *Never before have I seen*
> *such poor, shabby workmanship!*

he says, holding up
the suit Vijay made.

My mouth goes dry
when I see Baba and Vijay
standing before the crowd,
hands folded behind their backs,
heads bowed in shame.

Amma takes my hand
as Maya clutches the other.

At a glance, anyone can see
that Vijay's suit
is well-stitched and detailed
with good-length shirt cuffs,
a sharp cutaway collar,
and three gold buttons on the jacket,
just how Baba taught him.

General Chelmsford
holds it up like a rag
for the whole town to see.

> *You*, he bellows at Vijay,
> *are just like this suit!*
> *Clumsy, lazy,*
> *and a horrible mess.*

He turns to Baba.

I refuse to pay
for this ghastly garb
and will not be placing
any orders with you.

He and his officers
turn on their heels
and march off with Vijay's suit
through the parting crowd.

As people disperse,
we rush to Baba and Vijay.

Those thieves don't deserve
to wear our cotton on their backs,
Baba mutters,
patting Vijay's shoulder.

But my brother doesn't speak.

His eyebrows scrunch together,
nostrils flare, and eyes glower
in a way I've never seen before

and nobody eats
the kaju mithai.

NUMBERS

Each week Baba tries
to show me how numbers are
so easy
to understand.

His piercing eyes bore
deep
deep
deep
into mine

as if by staring hard enough
it will suddenly all make sense.

I nod when he asks
if I understand.
But the numbers swim to places
I cannot reach.
When he asks for the answer,
I stare blankly,
too scared to speak.

We sit in silence.

I ache to ask him
to come to the Kite Festival
so I can finally hear
those two
special words:

Dado sutho. Very good.

When he's proud of us,
Baba tells Vijay:
Dado sutho.

He tells Maya:
Dado sutho.

He tells me:

NIGHT WALLS

Night walls are thin.

He's different, Amma says.
Be patient.

He hasn't yet found
his strength.

> *Raj must be*
> *strong and smart*
> *to survive this world.*
>
> *Why is he scared*
> *of his own shadow?*
>
> *How can he be*
> *so weak in math,*
> *Baba asks,*
>
> *when Vijay is good with numbers*
> *and taking measurements*
> *and helping*
> *in our garment store?*
>
> *Even Maya gets*
> *better marks!*

And I squirm,
knowing my nine-year-old sister's ears
are sharp
and her head has just grown
a little bigger.

MAGIC

When math sums slide
out of my reach,
I secretly spy on Amma and Maya
blending red chilies, cinnamon sticks,
mustard seeds, and cloves,
the hissing and popping
sounds and scents
sending me

soaring
         flipping
                  spinning

as the thrill of
every stolen mouthful
twirls and sways on my tongue
and each speck of cumin
and tang of ginger, garlic, and onion
explode with flavor.

If Baba knew you were in here . . . ,
Amma says, catching me
by the ear.

> *Shh, Amma!*
> *I won't tell if you won't!*
> I throw a handful of spicy rice flakes
> and peanut chevra into my mouth
> and pinch a buttery nankhatai
> as she shoos me out.

MY TURN

It seems only fair
that every one of us
should be given a turn
to make magic.

I open my mouth,
then close it,
too scared to ask the question,
      knowing Baba would be happier
            if I asked to run wild and wrestle
                 with the rowdy boys outside

                  like Baba used to
                  like Vijay used to

                     but maybe when Baba
                     tastes the flavors
                     in my food,
                     he'll finally say,
                     Dado sutho.

I wait until Baba
has finished his chai,
then take a deep breath
and ask.

Mehrbani, Baba,
can I help make dinner today?
I've been watching Amma,
and I think I can remember
how to make moong dal

with spices, onions,
and tomatoes.

> You've been watching Amma?
> Baba asks.

Yes, and I'll even add
red chili powder just for you.

> So when you're supposed
> to be doing your math,
> which will give you the skills
> to join our tailoring business,
> you've been watching Amma?

I gulp.

> So now you know
> how to add chili powder
> but YOU CAN'T DO ALGEBRA?

His sharp glare
is like a painted sign
in bold letters
across the kitchen door:
No Boys Allowed.

SAGAR

Though my stomach
is growling,
I don't feel like eating breakfast.

Instead, I sit on my haunches
in our courtyard
and sulk.

Then I see our watchman, Sagar,
who has guarded our home
since he was old enough
to join his father,
who has guarded it since the time
he was old enough
to join his.

Sagar sits on his plastic chair,
logging details
of all the vehicles that pass,
and when I see him
twist his handlebar mustache,
searching our street for villains,
I can't help giggling.

I don't laugh for long, though,
because Vijay, who everyone thinks
is fast asleep,
suddenly appears
from behind a wall
wearing yesterday's clothes
and a bright glow.

He's holding hands with Bhavna,
but as soon as he sees me
he drops

his eyes
      her hand
            his smile

and doesn't say a word to me
the whole day.

VIJAY

Vijay walks around
like
a boiling pot of anger,
        a ticking time bomb.

He used to laugh
when we played,
shooting marbles, flying kites,
throwing his arm around me
whenever we walked home.

But he lost his smile
the day he lost faith in the British.
Now he only trusts his friends
Sham and Dhruv
and Dhruv's sister Bhavna.

Do you want to fly kites?

        I'm too old to fly.

Want to shoot some marbles?

        I don't have time.

Shall we play a game of cricket?
Or kabaddi or gilli danda?
I ask, grabbing the stick and block.

        I am needed
        for things that matter, Raj.

Though it's bad enough
he won't spend time with me,
what's worse is that
the only one he throws
his arm around,
her bed of curls bouncing,

is Maya.

MAYA

Since the moment
she could stand,
Maya tried her best to walk,
before she tried her best to run
after me.

Her footsteps
pat-pat-pattered down the stairs,
her pink dupatta flying
round and round
our marble dining table,
hands raised high.

It warmed my heart
to hear her squeal
whenever I scooped her up.

When I was eight
and she was five,
my baby sister giggled at
my paper crafts and tickles,
but soon, instead of craving just my time,
Maya took more interest
in taking
what
      was
           mine.

First, my spinning tops
hidden in her pockets.
Next, my pack of cards,
chewed and trampled,

s c a t t e r e d on the floor.
Then the final straw,
Maya solving puzzles,
winning card games,
complaining of tummy pain
after slurping up her milk,
and blinking those shiny brown eyes
to get whatever she desired,

including Baba's heart.

PROBABILITY

In the playground before school,
Tamir swipes a girl's satchel
and tosses it back and forth
with his friend, over her head.

Iqbal watches and sighs.
Then he places a rusted tin
on the wall
and aims with his slingshot.

The probability that I will
hit that tin is—

> *Higher than the probability*
> *of me passing the math test,*
> *I say, scowling.*

Come now, Raj, why don't you
have a turn shooting
to boost your confidence?

Iqbal hands me his slingshot.
I aim, pull back, and release the rock,
but instead of hitting the tin,
it shoots past the wall and into the playground,
grazing an ear.

> *Who shot that rock?*
> roars Tamir.

Now we bolt,
our legs pumping

around the wall and up the stairs
of the school building
to hide behind a pillar.

Tamir thunders after us,
but in his rage, he can't see straight
and races down the stairs again.

*Of all the ears at school
did you have to hit Tamir's?*
Iqbal whispers.

*I guess that probability
was also higher than me passing
the math test.*

LIGHTNING

Masterji sneers
as I squat and rise up,
again and again,
my fingers
pinching opposite earlobes,
my hands
bruised and swollen
from the lightning crack
of his wooden stick.

Doing this will improve
your concentration, Raj,
so that one day
you'll be smart
like your big brother.

Vijay smirks down at me
from Masterji's wall
as if he agrees,
and I grit my teeth, trying hard
not to think about
that probability.

PART II: GLIDING

LION

Like a bed of feathers,
the soft, sweet grass tickles my feet
as I take my white-and-blue lion
for a walk in the clouds.

At my command, he leaps to the sky,
yanking his tether, demanding more slack,
veering left then right,
climbing higher
as sunlight bounces off his tail.

My heart soars as my lion flies high
like it does at
Iqbal's laugh,
Amma's cooking,
and Nana's warm smile.

I tease the line this way and that,
turning my body to coax him
to follow my commands,
finding harmony with the wind
in letting out my string
and holding tight.

It's as though my lion
is an extension of my body
and my hand can touch
the sky.

In my bones, I know
that just like my lion, I, too,
am a roaring, soaring king

and when I win the Kite Festival,
Baba, Vijay, and Maya
will finally see the part of me
that can fly.

DON'T FORGET

I peek inside the kitchen,
inhaling the scent of garlic, mustard seeds,
green chilies, curry leaves,
and tomatoes from the seyal maani
Amma is preparing,
and tell her
I'm going to Iqbal's house.

Have a good time, she says,
but don't forget—

> *I know, Amma*, I say,
> stepping into the kitchen.
> *I can play with Iqbal,*
> *but I can't eat or drink*
> *the food in his home.*

I start to ask why
we can share our jokes,
our tricks, and even our dreams
but not our food and drink
when I hear
Baba's booming voice.

> *Raj! Is that you I hear*
> *in the kitchen?*

Before he appears,
I dart out the door
and decide to ask her
another time.

SECRETS

I stride right past
our watchman, Sagar,
and our courtyard gate,
to climb the hill to visit Iqbal.

His baba and ammi
are always glad to see me,
and they never talk
about math.

Now a weight presses
on my chest
as I remember the day
Iqbal offered me a sip
of his rose-scented milk
from their cow, Jana.

    I only remembered Amma's words
    when it was too late.

        When I saw how they loved
        their cow, Jana,
        just as we Hindus do,
        I decided it was all right
        to drink his milk and share food
        in secret.

        A secret at Diwali
        sharing my crunchy almond
        and pistachio varo
        with Iqbal.

A secret at Eid al-Fitr
sharing Iqbal's sweet bowl
of sheer khurma pudding
with me.

Each secret bringing us
closer,
making the treats taste
even sweeter.

GAME OF LUCK

Iqbal's home has no courtyard
or servants or even a watchman.
It only has two bedrooms
with a hut built
on the grass outside
for Jana.

Iqbal's baba is a fisherman,
casting a wide net each morning
and delivering his catch
to Baba's friend Uncle Bari,
who, according to Iqbal,
sells it at the market
for a much greater price
than what his baba gets paid.

When I visit, we play
Moksha Patam, a game of luck
on a board with gridded squares,
where we climb up ladders
and slip down snakes.

You're a lucky boy,
says his baba,
when I win the second time.

> *Raj is king,*
> Iqbal says proudly.

> > *Would the king like to learn*
> > *how to milk our queen, Jana?*
> > asks his ammi.

HALF A BUCKET

Crouching down
with shaking hands,
I reach for Jana's udder,
but she moves away.

Hurrying after her, I try again
as Iqbal holds his sides and chortles
when she won't stand still.
Even when I scratch behind her ears,
I only manage a squirt of milk
that shoots
straight in my eye.

Maybe this will help,
says Iqbal's baba,
placing a thick rope halter
around Jana's neck,
tying the lead to her post
as he gives her some grains
and hay to munch on.

Now she's still
as Iqbal and I take turns
pulling downward,
the right hand, then left,
from the base of her teats,
squeezing out
half a bucket of milk.

DREAM

Tonight I dreamed
  that my kite string
    cut into my skin,
      but I was brave
        and held on tight
          with a perfect pitch, roll, and spin.
            I won the Kite Festival
              and with the prize money,
                Iqbal and I opened a restaurant
                  where we shared
                    everybody's food,
                      even Jana's milk,
                        and Baba grinned so wide
                          with pride that I burst like a
                            plump, sweet
                              mango.

SAFFRON, WHITE, AND GREEN

Nana beams
and puffs out his chest
as he hands Iqbal and me
small tricolored flags.
The new flag of India,
for our country's independence.

It is saffron, white, and green,
but Nana says its true colors
are courage, faith, and peace.

The blue wheel
is the Ashoka Chakra.

Its twenty-four spokes
spin to remind us
there is life in movement
so we should welcome change,
says Nana.

> *How does a country*
> *become independent?* I ask.

By standing up
to other countries, like Britain,
and taking back its power
so it can start making
decisions for itself, he says.

It's a word I know well.
Baba is always telling me to be
more independent,

to tie my shoes,
to make my bed,
to get better marks.

And I wonder how long it will be
before I can make
Baba as proud
as Nana feels
about the Indian flag.

THE BRITISH RAJ

Why are the British Raj
leaving, Raj? Iqbal asks,
as we sway without a care
on Nana's jhoolo swing.

He grins that my name,
which also means ruler,
is used to describe the
British rulers of our land.

Nana sits down
on his charpai bedstead
to tell us about the man
he calls the father of India,
Mahatma Gandhi.

> *We have won our freedom*
> *through his nonviolent protests,*
> *with fasting and marching in peace.*

Iqbal and I
jump off the courtyard swing
and march around Nana.

> *By spinning our own khadi clothes*
> *and harvesting our salt,*
> *he also taught us how to save our money*
> *from greedy British fingers.*

Nana's dancing fingers
tickle our sides
till we laugh and squirm.

FREEDOM FIGHTERS

So India is becoming independent
because of Gandhi?
asks Iqbal.

> *Gandhiji, Nehru, and Jinnah,*
> *as well as freedom fighters*
> *like Sardar Patel and Bhagat Singh,*
> *have all played a part*
> *to help free India.*

Iqbal and I leap up,
pretend to be
freedom fighters,
shooting each other
and tumbling to the ground.

Are the freedom fighters
forcing the British to leave?
Iqbal asks,
as we lock hands
and wrestle.

> *Partly,* Nana says.

He tells us that the British
also lost money and soldiers
in the war,
so they can't afford to stay.

> In a hushed whisper
> he adds,
> *And they won't be missed.*

SEEING

As Amma and I dry papads
on our rooftop terrace
under the scorching sun,
I think about the British Raj.

Amma's pleated suthan pants,
cholo blouse, and draped dupatta
flutter in the breeze.

In the distance, I can see the walls
of our Pakko Qilo,
the old fort of Hyderabad,
and tell Ma
I will miss the British.

*After all, they've taught us
how to read and speak
in English.*

I point
to the train in the distance.
*They've made our railway
modern and efficient.*

I point
to our school.
*The officers at the gate
are friendly,
sharing their sherbet sweets
and not just on the queen's birthday.*

I'm a little sad
to see them go.

Wind thrashes
in the surrounding treetops,
and Amma pulls her dancing dupatta
around her.

She opens her mouth to speak,
but that's when I see
that Vijay has climbed
onto the terrace.

> You would not be sad
> if you knew what they have stolen,
> how they have treated us,
> burning our fingers to serve
> them phulko, while they burn
> our money and drink our chai.

I flinch, remembering how
Amma makes phulko,
bravely pinching its side,
flipping it faster than the flame
can lick her fingers
as the flatbread puffs up
like a balloon.

Now Vijay points
to the British-occupied bungalows
on the other side of town.

> They charge unfair taxes on salt,
> take the cotton, spices,

and crops from our land,
use the modern railways you boast of
to steal what is ours,
and sell it back at inflated prices.

Vijay's forehead creases.

> *They keep every last rupee,*
> *while our country starves,*
> *then look at us like we're*
> *uncivilized dogs,*
> *and you are sad to see them go?*

I swallow hard on something
that feels like a rock in my throat.

So this is why Gandhi says
the first step in freeing India
is wearing khadi.
By dressing in plain, homespun clothes,
we'll never need
to buy back our cotton
from the British.

And I see that there are
many things
I didn't see before.

SLUDGY MESS

I throw down my cards
as Maya wins
another canasta game.

Want to play again?
she asks, tossing her pink dupatta
over her shoulder.

And lose again? No thanks.

I know what we can do!

Maya's eyes light up.
She pulls me like a kite
into the kitchen.

Maya, I'm not allowed—

No one's home to catch you.

She blinks her shiny brown eyes
and before I know it
we are mixing atta flour and water
to make soft clay to play with.

She molds hearts and flowers
while I carve out kites and fish.
Then she climbs onto a stool,
scoops up a handful of atta flour,
and dumps it on my head.

This means war!

Atta flour balls
flit, glide, and fly
across the room
until we're covered
from head to toe
in a sticky, sludgy mess.

We giggle and roll
on the kitchen floor,
and though I know
I'll be in trouble
for giving in to her stubborn whims,
Maya squeals with such delight
I know it's worth it.

THIEVES

Maya and I sit on the stairs
listening
to Nana, Baba, and Vijay
complain about the British.

Before those thieves came,
we had one of the richest economies
in the world, says Baba.

        Vijay's shoulders slump.

        Now we're one of the poorest,
        most backward, and illiterate.

                They'll be gone soon enough,
                and we'll be free, says Nana.

As long as they don't
take any more from us
before they leave.

Nana has brought
sweet chikoos from the market
to share.

No, thanks, says Baba.
I'm not in the mood
for something sweet.

                Come now, says Nana,
                reaching for a fork.

Holding on to your anger
is like drinking poison
and expecting your enemy to
die.
We beat them in their own
game of cricket, didn't we?

Just have faith and we will be
victorious again.

CHIKOO

Maya scrambles down the stairs
and asks to eat Baba's share
of the sweet chikoos.

Of course you can,
my little chikoo, he says,
pulling her onto his knee
to feed her a piece.

> Can I have some too?
> I ask quietly.

Baba glances at me
and the twinkle in his eye
vanishes.

Raj, is it true
that the sticky mess
of atta flour and water
was made by you?

I lower my gaze and nod.

And did I not
make it very clear
that you are no longer allowed
in the kitchen?

I start to say that it was Maya,
but her large brown eyes
plead with mine.

Sorry, Baba,
it won't happen again,
I mumble, and go to my room.

Minutes later
our housemaid brings me
a bowl of fresh-cut chikoos,
but today, even Nana's favorite fruit
has lost its sweetness.

LOSER

Iqbal's kite
hangs like a star in the sky,
before a flurry of wind
sends it bucking
into a swoop, double-loop
CRASH.

You're a loser, Iqbal!
shouts Tamir, from beneath
a babul tree.

Use your kite for something
more useful, like killing flies!

I want to tell Tamir
to use his mouth for catching flies,
but his beefy build and tight fists
keep me silent as he snickers
and walks away.

When he's out of sight,
Iqbal lets out a frustrated grunt.

I am a loser, he's right.

You are not a loser, Iqbal.

I can't fly like you, Raj!
I'll never be the King of Kites.

My white kite
with its blue wheel

spins to a perfect finish.
I walk toward it,
lowering the tension in the line,
and as I reel it in, an idea strikes.

I'll be right back!

MANJHA

When I return,
Iqbal sits with a pout on his face
beneath the babul tree
and I can't help but grin.

What are you smiling at?

> *There will be two winners*
> *on the day of the Kite Festival.*

Yes, I know, the King of Kites
and the Kite Fighter.

I hand him a paper bag
with Vijay's kite string
coated with powdered glass.

> He peeks inside and gasps.

> Then he leaps up to embrace
> me.

Mehrbani, Raj.

He twists my nose.
I twist his back and we laugh.

SILVER PALLO

Nana and I sit by the water's edge
and dangle our feet
in the sparkling Indus.

Below us
fish dart and flit,
skimming the surface,
their scales glimmering in the sun.

*Do you know why
the silver pallo is my favorite?*
Nana asks.

I shake my head.

*Unlike most fish,
the pallo swims upstream
in a straight line,
against strong currents.*

I lick my lips,
remembering the rich, sweet aroma
of the pallo,
which sends hunger pangs
through my body.

*When it travels upstream
from places like Thatta,
it starts off black in color,*
he says, pointing to a black pallo.

But as it passes *Zinda Pir* shrine,
magic happens,
and it turns silver,
boasting a red spot on its head,
before returning home.

I think of the pallo we enjoy
every Saturday,
fried, steamed, cooked in curry,
or wrapped in muslin and roasted.

> *Is that why the silver pallo*
> *is so delicious, Nana?*

Yes, Raj.
A silver pallo
is brave, fierce, and strong enough
to survive a hard journey,
sometimes even a storm.

CUSTOM-MADE

Walking back from the river,
we hear shouts
from behind a cluster of trees,
and move closer
to see Vijay standing between
General Chelmsford and Bhavna.

You're mistaken, Vijay says.
Bhavna doesn't visit your side of town,
she's never met your wife,
and would never steal her scarf.

> *It was a gift from my mother, sir.*
> *Please don't take it*, pleads Bhavna,
> clutching the block-print fabric.

> *I said, hand it over now, you thief!*
> says the red-faced general.

Bhavna reluctantly surrenders
her scarf.

You are the thief! snarls Vijay.

> *What did you say?*

General Chelmsford
takes Vijay by the hair.

> *Kind general*, says Nana,
> stepping forward,
> *instead of this old cotton fabric,*

77

might I suggest,
as a gift to your wife,
a custom-made scarf
of the finest silk?

The general stops,
considers Nana's offer.
Yanking hard on Vijay's hair,
he pulls him so they're
nose to nose.

You're lucky Gramps is here
to save your neck.

He turns to Nana.

Have the fine silk sent
to my home tomorrow.

Then he releases Vijay
and walks away.

DEAL

Vijay and I
walk home in silence.

As we reach our courtyard,
he pulls me to one side.

We're not telling Baba
about what happened with
General Chelmsford.

       But why? It wasn't your—

If you keep quiet about today,
I'll help you with your math.
Deal?

Vijay extends his hand,
and as I clasp it
my heart leaps.

      Deal.

DIAMONDS

From our rooftop terrace
Vijay and I
release our kites.

My white and blue,
and his scarlet red,
soar and dip
liked colored diamonds
in an ocean of clouds.

Pointing at my rising lion,
Vijay describes
smaller triangles inside
imaginary squares
and then the formula
of $a^2 + b^2 = c^2$.

I laugh and ask my big brother
to show me more,
because time together,
with him teaching me
about points, lines, and coordinates,
is worth more than diamonds.

Even when my eyes squint tight,
the angles and shapes
that he describes
scatter into fragments across the endless sky
like infinite stars.

BAD OMEN

In the early morning,
Nana stands tall and lean,
feeding the sparrows
with rice, barley, and split peas
from the palm of his hand.

Your turn, Raj, he says,
cupping his hand to mine.
But just before a bird
swoops close enough,
I suck in my breath and
grains spill to the ground.

                    Watch me, says Maya,
                    quickly charming
                    a black-bibbed sparrow
                    into perching on her finger,
                    while three others
                    hop around her feet
                    to catch the falling seeds.

Nana's eyes shine
as he speaks
about monsoon rains of summers past.
The thrashing showers
that come in sheets,
punishing the windows nightly
and flooding our river Indus.

I scowl at the mention of rain,
which makes the earth
thick and muddy,

forming a giant puddle
under my favorite swing,
spitting and thundering
so my kite can't fly.

But with rain comes
new life, says Nana.
Rain brings cleansing
and renewal, he explains,
and always good fortune.

Now he stares with longing
at the sky above,
arms folded behind his back.

The rains are delayed this year,
a bad omen.

DANCING LEAF

Iqbal and I run
as our kites swoop and rise
like mighty emperors of the wind,
circling and circling
deep into the blue.

An excellent idea!
says Iqbal, laughing skyward
at the paper kites we made
to practice his line cutting.

>*You're ready, Iqbal!*
>*Now guide your line*
>*to cut down mine.*

You'll have to chase your kite
for miles after I slash you, Raj.
I'm moving in for the attack.
Are you ready?

>*Ready to be sliced!*

All of a sudden,
Iqbal slaps his forehead,
drops his wooden spool,
and takes off, leaving his kite
like a dancing leaf in the afternoon sun.

JANA

Where are you going, Iqbal?
I shout, reeling in both our kites
and rushing after him.

We reach his home,
where he dashes
toward Jana's hut.

Her white body
paces back and forth,
as she snorts and grunts.

Iqbal grabs the bucket
of grass, leaves, and stems
from corn and wheat,
tosses it into her feeding tray,
and pours water
into her empty bowl.

> *I've been so busy*
> *cutting down kites*
> *I forgot to feed her,*
> Iqbal says.

Jana drinks and chews
as Iqbal's eyes brim with tears.
He hands me the tiffin
from his sack, with his snack
of almonds and dates.

Jana didn't eat the whole day
because of me,
so now I won't eat either.

Iqbal bends forward
to stroke Jana's head.
He wraps his arms around her neck
and whispers,
Mukhe maaf kar, Jana.

After all that running,
my stomach is grumbling
and I lick my lips, imagining
the sweetness and crunch
from a handful of almonds
and juicy dates,
but I hand the tiffin back.

If you won't eat
for the rest of the day, Iqbal,
neither will I.

TREASURES

Hyderabad
is alive with color
as store vendors smile and wave,
with a pinch to my cheek,
or a pat on my head
and a piece of fruit
as I follow Baba
like I do each Saturday,
past the rush of dals,
seeds, rice, and beans
being poured into bags.

Short and stout,
Uncle Ghazi reaches on tiptoe
to pat my head in blessing
as we pass his cricket-bat stall.

*May you find many treasures
in the market today, Keshav!*

> *And may you sell
> many cricket bats, dear Ghazi!*
> Baba calls back.

I take in colorful, clinking bangles,
embroidered carpets and shawls,
melodies of flutes that charm
slithering snakes,
as bearded storytellers
gather crowds,
and almost feel sorry
for telling Maya that

we didn't have space to bring her
with us in the carriage today.

Almost.

BABA'S FRIEND

Uncle Bari
has been Baba's friend
since a day long before I was born,
when they learned
of their shared love of cards.

They meet each Friday
with Uncle Mitu and Uncle Ghazi
for tirpun games
lasting into the night,
when they sing
badly and out of tune
at the top of their lungs.

When a salwar suit was needed
for Uncle Bari's nephew's wedding,
his family of fifty
and all the wedding guests
queued proudly outside Baba's store.

And when we crave
our spicy fish pallo,
which is every single Saturday,
Uncle Bari's fish stall is the
only place we go.

Welcome, old friend!
What fun we had last night
and how I enjoyed my beef biryani,
though I had more luck singing
than playing tirpun.

Are you sure about that, Bari?
You sounded rather awful!
says Baba with a chuckle,
slapping Uncle Bari on the back.

Oh, you wound me, Keshav.
Uncle Bari plunges a pretend dagger
into his chest and winks.

Look, I saved
my fattest silver pallo
just for you.

Baba tries to pay
but Uncle Bari stops him.

Next time, next time,
he says,
wrapping the fish
with a smile and wave.

SWEETEST TREAT

The market heaves
with sweets
served for celebration:
syrupy-crisp coiled jalebis,
silver-foiled kaju mithai,
creamy pista barfi,
all in the colors of
saffron, white, and green,
just like the Indian flag.

It's the happiest time in
India's history, Raj.
Would you like a treat?

My mouth falls open.

Baba *never* stops for sweets.

I nod with a grin,
choosing a tall glass of icy falooda,
so Baba will sit with me
in the shaded stall,

not Vijay,
        not Maya,
                just me,

as I drink the rose syrup milk
with basil seeds,
the long strands of vermicelli
slipping down my throat.

HAPPY TUNE

From the corner of my eye
I catch Baba smiling.

Baba, you know the
Independence Day Kite Festival?

>*Of course, Raj,*
>*the whole town is talking about it.*

Well . . . I'm planning to enter
and win!

>*That's my boy!*
>*You can use Vijay's sharp*
>*and strong manjha—*

No, I don't mean
the Kite Fighting Competition
that you and Vijay both won.
I want to be named the King of Kites.
Will you come to watch?

But Baba is already watching
a toothless vendor
singing his favorite song,
"Dama Dam Mast Qalandar,"
as he sells embroidered shawls.

Baba? I ask again.

>*Whether or not you are named*
>*King of Kites, son, I'll be there.*

As Baba hums the happy tune,
I see people of every age
waving our new tricolored flag
of saffron, white, and green,
and it makes me glow
with happiness inside.

Because just like Baba,
it seems
with independence coming
nothing can ever
upset India again.

PART III: SPIRALING

THE LINE

Sometimes Baba comes home late,
after he's had a whiskey
and a smoke from the hookah pipe
with his friends
in Uncle Mitu's special room,
where only men go.

Amma waits up for him.
Maya and I huddle on the stairs
so we can also hear
the "local news," which is
far more reliable
than the radio broadcasts
from the new viceroy.

Tonight, Baba's hands
twist and turn
as his wide eyes droop.

He says when the British leave,
India will be sliced in two.

Broken,
by a line to be drawn
on a map
by a British man.

For what? Amma asks.
And how can anyone draw a line
between neighbors?
        between brothers?
                between friends?

I think about the lines
we draw every day,
lines of shapes,
lines to add, subtract, and multiply,
lines for games like hopscotch,
but it sounds like the line
this British man is going to draw
on a paper map
is not like these.

Baba tugs his bottom lip
and says
he doesn't know for sure
where the line on the map
will be drawn.

> *The British man*
> *who's never been to India*
> *is coming*
> *for the very first time,*
> *and he will decide.*

WILL HE SEE?

My throat itches
with a question.

If a British man is coming here
for the
very first time,
how can it be that he can see
where this line should be drawn?

When he draws it,
will he see
the lines etched into my
mango tree?

The lines on the faces
of our ancestors
who have lived in Sindh
for centuries?

The lines of the railway track
that the British built to carry
our spices and cotton and wealth
far away?

Will he see
we already have
lines of memory,
     lines with meaning,
          and that maybe
               we don't need
                    another line
                         after all?

WHEN I HEAR IT

I am halfway down the stairs.

Are you sure, son?

> *Yes, Baba,* says Vijay.
> *One of my clients*
> *said the line the British man will draw*
> *will divide*
> *not young and old,*
> *men and women,*
> *or rich and poor*
> *but . . .*

I freeze,
straining to hear
Vijay whisper to Baba.

Hindus,
>   *Sikhs,*
>>   *and Muslims.*

My knuckles turn white
from gripping our banister,
and my throat tightens.

My thoughts fly to Iqbal,
and the word

divide

slowly settles
in

my

gut

as Iqbal

and even his kite,

feel like they're   being   pulled   far   away.

BOUNDARY LINES

Nana is not himself
as we sit face-to-face,
in our weekly battle,
across the carrom board.

He is not one to miss
the black or white disk,
which he flicks
with calculated aim,
potting them in one of four nets
on each corner of the board.

His eyes scan the
boundary lines
where his striker can sit
as he considers his next move.

I know from the way
his forehead wrinkles,
like Baba's when he's cheated
by a fabric supplier,
that his mind is fixed
on a very different line.

Strike after strike
my disks go in,
even the queen, gliding easily
across the powdered board.

When I win and glance up,
beaming wide with surprise,
I see his eyes

fixed on the window,
hungry more than ever
for the stubborn rain.

I realize it is not so much
that I am winning,
but that Nana is playing
in a way that says
he has already lost.

BOULDERS

Along the bank of the Indus,
where mosquitoes hum overhead,
Iqbal and I hurl sticks
across the water.

We pick flat stones
and take turns
tossing, so they'll skip,
one,
       two,
              three times
across the water's surface.

Usually, my words come out
babbling
like running water.
But now my words feel
heavy as boulders
and Iqbal is so quiet
I know he's heard too
and doesn't know
what to say.

We laugh and point
at one another
when the stones plop hard and sink,

like

my

words

before they can be spoken,
way
      way
            down

     below.

Sometimes, it's easier just to laugh
and push each other
into the cool of the swell
and not talk about the thing
weighing
on both of our minds.

THRASHING

When Iqbal and I
are soaked through,
together our fingers
follow a slippery silver pallo.

Hands close in and clasp tight,
as we thrust it
high above the water.

As our prize squirms,
its body thrashing in wild panic,
Iqbal's eyes meet mine,
and without a word
we set it free.

I know that
Iqbal's baba and ammi
have told him the same story
that Nana told me—
that a silver pallo
is known for being
brave, fierce, and strong enough
to survive a hard journey,
sometimes even a storm.

I also know that the pallo
is a fish
that, at least today,
has earned its freedom.

BULLET

Before school,
Tamir walks onto the playground,
snatches the food tiffin
of a boy half his size,
and taunts him till he cries.

Then rocks fly
one
        by
               one
from Iqbal's slingshot
behind our wall.

Dropping the tiffin,
Tamir moves like a bullet
off the playground, up the stairs,
leaping behind the pillar
to catch Iqbal by
the neck.

Did you really think
I wouldn't know
it was you, cousin?
he growls.

        Mukhe maaf kar, Tamir.
        Mehrbani . . . , chokes Iqbal,
        his face purple.

This better be the last time
you meddle,

or I might just forget
we're related.

Tamir shoves Iqbal
to the ground
and kicks him hard.

CATCHING THE CLOUDS

Wait! I call,
rushing after Iqbal as he runs
to the park behind the school
so that no one can see
his face is wet.

He perches
on his favorite swing,
turning away, still sobbing
as I silently sit on mine
and push off.

> *I hate him so much, Raj!*
> *I wish you were my cousin*
> *instead of Tamir.*

I wish you were my brother.
Then I'd teach you how to fly
like I'm flying now.

Iqbal turns to me with half a smile.

> *You're barely floating, Raj.*

Oh really?
Well, I bet you can't
catch the clouds before me, brother!

> *Bet I can, brother!*

In five minutes
we are laughing again

in the tickling breeze,
pushing off harder,
feet
swinging
rocking
gliding

                         higher

            higher

higher
into the sky
as we leap off
our swings
to catch the clouds.

PARTITION

Masterji waves his wooden stick
when he says, *School will close
for one whole week!*

The class cheers, breaks into chatter
about how everyone will celebrate
the greatest event in history.

He clears his throat

and says that after independence,
India will also divide
into two separate states.

*The last viceroy of India,
Lord Mountbatten,
has agreed to a boundary line
that will break our country into two.*

He's calling it Partition.

And the silence
that falls across the room
is the loudest sound of all.

CHOPPED

Why does India
have to be divided?
asks a voice from the back.

Masterji's shoulders sink.

> *It is believed*
> *we will be happiest*
> *living in our own religious groups.*

Though from his strained face
it does not seem
like Masterji believes this.

He explains that
with fewer Muslims
in India,
Jinnah—leader of the Muslim League—
has asked for their own state,

> *to make sure they're treated fairly*
> *after independence.*

> *What about Gandhiji?* I ask,
> remembering the small, bald man
> in his white dhoti pants and
> spectacles,
> who won our freedom fight
> not with weapons and words
> but with peaceful marches
> and fasts.

Gandhiji wants a united India,
not a partitioned one,
but after many disagreements
between the Indian National Congress
and the Muslim League,
the British have agreed
to slice our country into two.

So, India will split down the
middle, like an apple?
Iqbal asks.

I can imagine
Sindh in the shape of an apple.
Even chopped down the middle,
with its seeds falling
to either side of its center,
Iqbal and I could happily live
only minutes apart.

Masterji interrupts my thoughts,
saying it will be up to
each family to choose
whether or not they want to move.

Then Iqbal's face lights up.
So if no one moves,
nothing will change,
In shaa Allah?

MANGO TREE

On our way back from school,
I scramble up our mango tree,
the very same one
Iqbal taught me to climb,
years ago.

From up so high
Sindh seems small,
yet the world feels large,
like there's more to see beyond
the borders of Hyderabad.

From up so high
I spy my brother Vijay,
huddling with Bhavna,
Dhruv, and Sham,
in a secret meeting.

I know he has secrets,
from the times he's snuck
out of the house,
not saying a word
or meeting my eyes
after he comes back.

Now I have
a bird's-eye view
of the crate they're prying open
with a crowbar.

The crate looks like it holds
a secret stash of ripe,

juicy mangoes,
plump with promise,
like the future of India.

My mouth waters,
as Bhavna and Sham lift the lid,
before Dhruv and Vijay
pull back a gray blanket.

I blink twice
and squint to be sure
I'm seeing what I'm seeing:
a pile of long blades
and shiny black pistols,
and I can't stop
my scream.

PROTEST

Vijay glares up at me.

At first, he doesn't answer
when I scramble down my tree
to ask
where he got them,
          why he needs them,
                    since independence is a celebration.

He only speaks when I promise
I won't tell.

They're for just in case, he mutters.
The rocks we throw and signs we paint
aren't enough to win the protest
against Partition.

The divide that General Chelmsford
and the British
have no right to make.

If Vijay can stop it, I'll be glad,
though I worry
that his idea of protests
isn't the same as Gandhiji's protests,
with fasting, singing, and peace.

Now the sour taste of metal
fills my mouth
when I think of his crate,
not filled with sweet, ripe fruit
but sharp and deadly weapons.

DRAWING BLOOD

My mind races
with all I've seen and heard,
but I know I cannot tell
what Vijay shared,
so I drink the bitter taste
of worry and say,

I'm home!

A welcome scent
wraps around me.
I inhale Amma's crisp sambosas
sizzling in the sputtering oil
and the scent of her
zesty mint chutney.

Maya's plate is licked clean
as she moves to pinch
one of my sambosas.

Ne kar! I shout, reaching forward
as she stuffs the hot parcel
into her cheeky mouth,
before smirking
and loudly slurping her milk.

Maya springs like a cat
onto the counter, eager to share
before I do
that school will be closed
for the independence celebrations.

And maybe nothing
will change, I add,
when the borderline is drawn.

Baba appears from nowhere,
his dusty tunic stained
with long streaks of brown.

I tell him that even when
the line is drawn,
families can still choose to stay.

I hope the news will please him,
that he'll finally say,
Dado sutho, very good,
but his eyes are firm
like there's a math test
to study for.

Now I notice his tousled hair
and wonder why
he's home two hours early.

With shaky hands,
Baba tells us about the accident
near his garment store.

> The Mirza brothers
> waged war over land
> with Moti Laghari.
> He ordered them to leave,
> and they responded
> by drawing their swords.

Amma gasps.

Is he . . .

Baba's eyes silence Amma.

Sadly, he shakes his head
and says,

The drawing of this line
is drawing blood on the streets.

MADNESS

Amma pretends to receive
what Baba says calmly,
but her wild eyes
betray her.

Perhaps Sindh will be fine,
like Punjab and Bengal—
an equal Hindu-Muslim divide.

> Baba says nothing
> is ever equal.
>
> *I've heard too much on the radio*
> *about the bloodshed*
> *and riots in Calcutta,*
> *the looting and fires*
> *in Delhi and Amritsar.*
>
> *They're acting like animals,*
> *and all we can do*
> *is hope and pray*
> *the madness*
> *won't spread to us.*

Maybe everything
will settle with the new
borderline?

> *That borderline will be*
> *the biggest reason to fight—*
> *that line is why*
> *I'm most afraid.*

I see lines
        everywhere I turn:
            the line of a knife,
                the line of a bullet from a gun.
                I can even draw a line between
                    Amma's and Baba's eyes,
                    locked on each other,
                        having an entire conversation
                        without exchanging
                            a single word.

                    Then Maya cries out,
                    breaking the silence,

                    Look!
                    The sambosas—they're all burnt!

TRICOLORED

Our bright kites
leap and dive in the sky
like playful fish
and I think about the things
Vijay shared, about the changes
coming to Sindh.

Ready to win
the Kite Festival, Raj?
asks Iqbal.

> Before, I would raise my chin
> at my kite spinning in the breeze,
> but now the air around me
> feels heavy.
>
> *Will everything be the same*
> *after independence?*

Iqbal twists my nose.
I twist his nose back.

> *What if something*
> *bad happens? I ask.*

Nana is watching us today
and answers my question
with a question.

> *Did you know*
> *that a kite rises highest*
> *when it flies against the wind?*

I glance up,
see that Nana is right.
My lion lifts as it resists the wind,
rising higher each time.

The kites bounce high
in the breeze,
following each other,
climbing and falling through the clouds,
until the two kites seem to
merge into one.

If I look carefully
and stretch my imagination,
ever so slightly
when Iqbal's
saffron-and-green patang
meets my white kite, with its wheel of blue,
they look a little like
the saffron, white, and green
tricolored flag.

Together they paint a picture
of India,
saffron, white, and green,
flying up and up,
free and victorious
forever.

SPARROWS

I arrive early at Nana's home
and am surprised to see him leaving
with a large bundle of branches
balanced on his head.

Where are you going, Nana?
I'd like to try to feed
the sparrows again.

> *Not today, Raj,*
> *I am needed this morning.*
> *The sparrows will have to wait.*

Who needs you?
I'm very good at building things.
I can come too.

> *No, Raj.*
> *You cannot come with me today.*
> *Why don't you practice*
> *your kite tricks, and I'll be back soon.*

I practice my tricks,
shoot marbles,
build card towers under the sun,
and even pick two pocketfuls of blackberries
but can't help wondering
what Nana is doing.

Is he building a fortress?
A wall? Or a gate?
To help keep us safe?

The sun goes down
and there's a chill in the breeze
when Nana returns.

I step behind a bush
so he won't see that
I've waited all day.

Nana's feet drag slowly.
He wipes the sweat
from his head and neck,
his shoulders bowed,
his chest exposed,
with his kurta top missing.

Suddenly he stops.
His eyes clench
and he lets out a moan
as his chest heaves and falls.

At first, I am sure
that Nana is laughing,
and I almost run out
to share in his joke.
But then I see,
for the very first time,
my nana softly cry

and even the sparrows
stay silent.

STRONGER TOGETHER

Amma has two best friends—
Bhavna and Dhruv's mother,
Aunty Neelam,
and Sham's mother,
Aunty Sundri.

Each week the three meet
to play rummy,
and it's far more entertaining
to listen to them than do math.

I've been hearing things, says Amma.

Aunty Neelam, known
for being a gossip, leans forward.

*I think there might be more attacks
like the one that killed Moti Laghari.*

Aunty Sundri's eyes widen
because her husband, Uncle Nanik,
isn't here to protect her from more
attacks.
He's a Sindhworki, living abroad,
selling gold and silk embroideries in
Cairo.
      Do you think we should leave Sindh?

             *And go where? This is our home.
             It is our birthright to stay!*
             shouts Aunty Neelam.

Neelam's right.
I'm sure the tensions will settle
with time, says Amma.

It is us against the British,
not each other.
With independence coming,
let's not worry. Let's celebrate!

Maybe our feasting and dancing
will remind every
Hindu, Sikh, and Muslim
that we are one brotherhood,
says Aunty Sundri.

Stronger together.

Always, says Amma with a nod.

INDEPENDENCE

At the stroke of midnight,
India will become a free nation.

Like an eagle,
it will rise, it will soar
and fly bold and free.

But Viceroy Mountbatten
can't be in Karachi and New Delhi
at the same time, says Iqbal.
Baba says our celebrations begin
the moment Mountbatten
transfers power to Pakistan.
Today is also the twenty-seventh day of Ramadan.
It is very auspicious.
So we will celebrate today
and you'll celebrate tomorrow.

It seems so strange that
we're celebrating
the birthday of our motherland
on different days.

I want you to come today, Raj,
but Ammi says it's not a good idea.

> *I asked if you could come tomorrow*
> *but Amma said the same.*

I wish we could enjoy
our country's independence
together.

I think for a minute
and an idea forms in my mind.

Maybe we can!

STAR AND CRESCENT

I'm hiding
under Iqbal's back window,
scooping up tiny stones to throw.
Clink-clink-clink.
They let him know
I'm here.

From his window
I hear laughter and feasting
with shouts of Quaid-i-Azam, great leader,
as Radio Pakistan
replays a recitation of the Holy Quran
and Muhammad Ali Jinnah's speech
about the dawn of freedom.

Then a chanting
of *Pa-ki-stan Zin-da-bad* grows loud
and friends and family
spill out of Iqbal's home,
falling into a line that marches
through the streets,
waving green-and-white
star-and-crescent flags
as they share sweets
with their community.

I creep toward Jana's hut,
making sure no one sees.

Iqbal is waiting with a plate
of sesame-seed-paste halva
crunchy baklava pastries,

and qatayef dumplings
drizzled with sweet sugar syrup
and powdered sugar.

I share my bowl
of carrot halwa pudding,
cardamom-flavored besan-flour ladoos,
and milk-based almond and pistachio barfi
decorated with edible silver foil.

As a treat for Jana,
so she can also celebrate,
I've brought apples and carrots.

She nuzzles her head next to mine,
making me giggle
as her warm breath
tickles my neck.

Before eating,
Iqbal and I say a prayer of thanks,
his hands cupped
my hands folded.

Our eyes shine bright
as the three of us
gobble our treats with relish.

Then I stop.

I came to celebrate
your independence, Iqbal.
How will you join me
to celebrate mine?

He taps his chin,
then places his hand on my shoulder.

Don't worry, Raj.
I'll find a way.

CELEBRATION

Music blares
as family and friends
from every stage of my memory
pour into my home to join our
Independence Day celebration.

Uncle Mitu, Aunty Neelam,
and Aunty Sundri
chat and smoke on rickety chairs,
others toast with thadal and sharbat.
Vijay, Bhavna, Dhruv, and Sham
devour the spinach-and-vegetable curry,
lotus root in onion gravy,
and crunchy kheechas.

I long to ask Nana
what he's building
with the branches I've seen him carry,
but as Maya lets out a whistle
at the towering stack of phulko,
I decide now isn't the time.

Nana and Maya
take at least two helpings
of each delicious sweet,
but I'm too full
to try one more bite
of the sugar-rich, nutty mithai.

BUBBLING

Nana leads us in a dance
around our dining table.
Maya skips and twirls,
her little flag
swoops and climbs,
and I remember how Iqbal's kite and mine
met together in the sky
to form a picture of the very flags
we're holding.

Nana calls us to stand around him,
saying that today we're going to sing
a new anthem
instead of "God Save the King."

It's called "Vande Mataram"—
"I Praise Thee, Mother."

Let's salute and rejoice
in our motherland's freedom.
She isn't going to be told
what to do anymore.

A bubbling sensation rises inside,
and it isn't just
saffron, white, and green
but bubbles of every color
that float from the tip of my toes
to the top of my head.

I stand next to Vijay,
who is hard to recognize
when he's beaming.

I raise a stiff hand to my brow
and sing with my whole heart.

HAPPY BIRTHDAY

At eleven o'clock
we switch on All India Radio
to listen to the speeches of India's leaders.

Nana's eyes sparkle
as Prime Minister Nehru gives
his "Tryst with Destiny" speech.

At the stroke of the midnight hour . . .

Amma's smile doesn't reach her eyes,
and her eyebrows scrunch tight.

when the world sleeps . . .

Vijay stands tall and resolute,
his chest puffed out.

India will awake to . . .

Maya wears an impish grin
and bounces on her stool.

life and freedom.

Baba's fingers stroke his watch
before he wipes his eyes.

Nana rises.

He wishes the British troops
a safe journey home

and raises his whiskey glass
to the Indian flag being raised above
the Lahori Gate of the Red Fort.

And in a voice that
partly sings, partly shouts,
and is partly choked,
Nana says,

Happy birthday, Mother India!

FIREWORKS

BOOM! BOOM! BOOM!

Running out onto the streets,
we join with other families
in rhythmic chanting,
Hin-du-stan Zin-da-bad!
as fireworks throw colors
across the night sky.

Scarlet waterfalls flow from above,
whisking lines of color
that shatter into a thousand sparks,
and through the dark,
I can just make out
Nana and Maya
punching arms to the sky
and together we shout,
Bharat Mata ki Jai and *Mother-free,*
as silver showers splatter above.

Raj, shouts a voice
in the pitch blackness.
I feel an arm link with mine.
I smile without needing to turn,
for I know who's standing
by my side,
who'll drift upon paper wings
to touch the stars with me
and stand beside me
my entire life.

BREWING

Overnight
something shifts in the wind.

The rains haven't come,
yet the howls sound
like a brewing storm.

As the British troops leave,
quarrels grow between
Baba's friends, my "uncles,"
over little things, like not returning
a bullock cart or not seeing eye to eye
on the price of a woven rug.

That first morning
after independence,
there's a brawling in the road,
over the milk wallah.

Uncle Mitu blocks his path,
warns him not to deliver
to Uncle Bari's home.

Bari—that Muslim—slaughters cows.
He doesn't deserve to drink
their sacred milk.

I can't understand
why this matters now:
Uncle Bari has always
eaten beef.

NOT FOR SALE

It is five days
since the
independence celebrations
and eight more days
till the Kite Festival.

Baba points to a fat,
glistening silver pallo
at Uncle Bari's stall,
and I lick my lips,
remembering the tang
of chili garlic, coriander, and cumin.

Not for sale, Uncle Bari says,
in a voice thick as gravy.

> *How about that black one then?*
> asks Baba.

Uncle Bari pauses.

Not for sale, Uncle Bari says again.
NOTHING IS FOR SALE!

Now his voice sounds
like a sharpened blade.

My father stares at his friend
as surprise,
    then understanding,
        and finally anger
        wash over him.

YOUR KIND

What are you doing,
old friend? asks Baba.

> *We are not serving*
> *your kind anymore.*

My father's face swells with color.

OUR KIND?
Baba roars
with the force of thunder.

I take a step closer
but don't dare touch
Baba's trembling arm.

Never before
have I seen my father
so flustered
that he cannot speak.

He stares at the ground,
and with a hand on my shoulder,
he guides me away
from his old friend's stall.

WHO IS SAFE?

As we move through the market,
I take in more stares.

A look, a word, a shove
could spark a fire.

For the first time, I register
Baba's friends by their:

Gandhi caps,   pagris,   and topis.

Even the women
move with suspicion,
in groups:

of dupatta-draped suthan-cholo,

           dupatta-draped shalwar kameez,

              and chador-draped koti-paro.

I start a list in my head
of who are:

Hindu,   Sikh,   and Muslim

so I can tell who is safe,
and who, overnight,
is not safe anymore.

RUMORS

On our next visit
to the market,
we stop only at the stalls
of friends who are Hindu and Sikh,
but Uncle Ghazi,
near the end of the market,
beckons to us
with a merry wave.

It is ten days since the
independence celebrations
and three more days
till the Kite Festival.

I am surprised
you don't hate us too, Baba says,
with injury in his voice.

> *Ah, but how can I hate you*
> *when we have played as babies?*
> Uncle Ghazi says,
> with a chuckle that makes
> his whole middle wobble.

> *It is just silly rumors,*
> *about the new borderline.*

He pats my arm,
tells me not to worry,
but his wringing hands
and eyes that dart from left to right
say something different.

CRICKET BAT

Baba chuckles
and points
to Uncle Ghazi's empty shelf,
where one cricket bat remains.

Well, at least I see,
you have done well.

In a flash, the light
in Uncle Ghazi's eyes
is gone
and he draws us close.

> *Take this bat, he says.*
> *I kept it for my own protection,*
> *but it is my gift to your son.*
> *Tamir and his gang*
> *have stolen from my stall*
> *and aren't afraid to use*
> *the nineteen other bats.*

> *May Allah protect you.*

My throat tightens
just thinking about Tamir
and his gang of nineteen.

The bat is light in my hands,
but also heavy in ways
I have no words for.

I try to push it back at Uncle,
but he only presses it harder
into my hands.

                              Baba..., I plead.

Take Uncle's gift, he says.

                              I can never use this to—

Then give it to Vijay,
or better still, give it to Maya.

She won't be afraid to use it.

WHAT I KNOW

Lines,
        lines,
                lines.

Kite strings are long lines,
stitches by tailors are little lines,
multiplication and equal signs in math are crossed or parallel
lines,
and railroads
                stretch
                        into the longest lines for miles and
                        miles and miles.

If you break a kite string, it's bad,
    if the stitches break, it's bad,
        if you can't calculate, it's bad,
            if you block a railroad, it's bad.
                I may not know very much
                    about the line this British man is drawing,
                    but I do know one thing.

                    It's bad.

CHANGE

Nana and I walk
beside the river Indus.

Everything is changing, I say.

> *Change is good,* he replies,
> pointing to the pallo,
> which changes from black to silver
> when brave enough
> to face a hard journey.

I'm not brave like the pallo,
and you, Nana.
I'm afraid.

> *Being brave doesn't mean*
> *you're not afraid, Raj.*
> *It means doing the*
> *right thing anyway.*

But what if something
bad happens?

Nana ponders my question
as we plop down onto
the riverbank,
under the shaded date palms,
dangling our feet together
in the cool water.

Remember when
your kite is impossible to control,
and the string even cuts into your hand,
there's only one thing to do, right?

Nana grins.

Hold on tight!
we say together.

Soon the wind
will change in your favor,
just as long as you
don't let go.

PART IV: FALLING

WHISPERS

Late one night
when stars twinkle, crickets chirp,
and Sagar patrols
outside our courtyard wall,
Vijay and his friends
speak in whispers.

They do not see me tiptoe close
to the wall behind
which they share
all their secrets.

It is twelve days since the
independence celebrations,
and the Kite Festival
is tomorrow.

Are you sure?
Bhavna asks.

> *How can it be*, asks Dhruv,
> *when Sindh has more*
> *Muslims than Hindus?*

> *Hindus and Sikhs*
> *own more of the land,*
> *so we can stay,*
> *but our Muslim brothers*
> *will have to leave*, says Vijay.

I reach for the wall
as my knees buckle.

But we've lived side by side
with Muslims for centuries,
says Bhavna.

Can't we share Sindh?

                              We can and we will.

                              When our Muslim brothers
                              see us marching, shouting,
                              and waving signs to help them stay,
                              they will surely join in,
                              and together we will overpower
                              the British generals, forcing them
                              to put an end to Partition.

                              And with the Kite Festival,
                              no one will be expecting us.

TOMORROW

Tomorrow is
the Kite Festival—
my chance
      to win
      and show Baba
      and everyone
           that I am brave
           and strong
              and king of something.

Tomorrow is also the protest—
our chance
      to win
      and show Iqbal
      and our Muslim brothers
           that we are brave
           and strong
              and want them to stay.

I want more
than anything
to
soar and dip
      twist and flip
           feel the f r e e d o m
of the breeze
and win . . .

but what good
is winning
without Iqbal?

SPINNING

My head throbs
from a million spinning thoughts,
from tossing and turning
all night long.

Did I dream
what I think I heard?
Or will Iqbal and his family
really have to leave Sindh
forever?

Where will he go?
        What will he take?
                Will I ever see him again?

By the morning,
worry and fear
swim together in my stomach
and I rush downstairs to tell
the only person who will know
what to do.

But Nana's not there.

What is it, Raj?

I open my mouth
but my words are stuck,
and with his usual sigh,
Baba waves me away.

I know I must be brave
and help win this protest
so that Iqbal can stay.

I fetch my kite, then stop,
put it back, take a breath,
and reach
for my cricket bat instead.

KITE FESTIVAL

I fly
past the just-watered jasmine bush,
but instead of turning right,
I can't resist a detour
through the main square,
jumping over a gate and around the back
of the market tower
to the Kite Festival,
where kites of every color
swish their magnificent tails
and soar like colored birds set free.

As they flap and glide,
climbing to the crest of gusts and pulls,
I feel a knot in my gut
for missing the chance
of kingship.

Now I see Iqbal,
his kite sailing high,
eager to cut down
the other swirling kites.

Raj! Where are you going?
shouts Iqbal.

                    You'll see!

He stands frozen
in disbelief.

I laugh with a wave
and dash through the crowds,
thrusting my cricket bat high,
imagining how grateful and relieved
he'll be
when I tell him that instead
of winning the Kite Festival,
I stopped Partition.

Now the fastest way to Vijay
is through the narrow left lane
past the mosque.

Though Baba's warned me
not to walk this way, he never said
I couldn't run.

SINGLE EYE

Hindu or Muslim? asks a woman
who is guarding the mosque.
She is fully draped
in a white chador,
revealing only a single eye
that pierces mine.

I stop,
my heart beating in my throat.

Even as I take off
along the unpaved trail,
I feel several men
and chador-draped women
set eyes on me.

Darting through a lane
of vendors with wares,
I pump my legs as the sound
of chase grows loud,
moving forward
in the direction of the protest
outside General Chelmsford's home.

SWARM

I dip my head
and grip my bat,
feeling pleased that I've lost them,
imagining Vijay's surprise
and pride when he sees

I am brave
      and fierce
            and strong
            as a silver pallo.

Strong enough to join his protest, like him.

Now I hear a thundering of feet
and turn to see
a swarm of angry Muslims
behind me.
They see my brother and his friends
holding guns and knives
and think I've led them to an . . .
ambush!

Suddenly there are screams,
accusations flying
about this trap, an attack,
and my brother isn't smiling,
but trembling as he drops his gun
and cries in panic,

RAJ, RUN!

I duck under a paved bridge,
around the back of the slanted wall,
my legs and heart pounding
as the trees hurry me along,
their swaying branches
beckoning me like arms.

GUILT ROLLS HEAVY

I hear a deafening roar,
see a wave of fists
as sharp blades flash
and bullets slice the air.
I dump my bat and let
my hands and feet take me
where they usually do,
scrambling up a mango tree.

Panting hard, I peer down
through branches.
Branches that need to
protect me because
I am NOT brave
        or fierce
        or strong like the silver pallo.

My chest heaves
with sobs
and silent regret.

Guilt rolls heavy
down my spine
as I watch the mob of men
raising their fists and cursing
Vijay's guns and knives—
now used in defense
against the very people
they were trying
to protect.

BROKEN

Vijay raises his hands
in surrender.

He moves slowly
toward the crowd,
his arms whirling
as he explains about the protest.

The protest that he,
Dhruv, Bhavna, and Sham
are leading to stop Partition
so our Muslim brothers
can stay.

Now a gang of boys
with cricket bats
cuts through the crowd.

Their leader is Tamir,
who charges to the front,
stirring up
a ripple of angry words
that punctures the air like arrows.
Then Tamir goes wild
with his bat,
swinging in all directions.

Vijay calls
to General Chelmsford,
pleading for him to
stop the chaos,
but the red-haired general

only smirks, shakes his head,
and leads his team of officers
back into his home.

Suddenly, Tamir swings
his bat at Bhavna,
smacking her across the head,
and Vijay fights back.

Tamir swings his bat again.
Vijay ducks, grabs it,
and tosses it away.
Tamir flicks open
a silver blade.
They dance back and forth,
standing high, squatting low,
moving round and round
until Tamir lunges forward,
slashing Vijay's arm.

Vijay charges at Tamir,
knocking him down to the ground
leaping on top of him
and twisting his arm,
punching
            and punching
until Tamir's arm
looks broken.

GOOSE BUMPS

When it starts to get dark,
I climb back down
the mango tree,
find my cricket bat,
and creep along in the shadows
as I make my way home.

I nod to Sagar,
tiptoe through our courtyard,
but as I reach the main door,
I stand face-to-face
with broad-shouldered,
      arms-folded,
           foot-tapping
               Baba.

He makes that face
where his muscles are tight and twisted
with disappointment.

*I came to watch you win
the Kite Festival
and be named the King of Kites.*

I bite my lip.

*Then I met Uncle Mitu,
who told me about Bhavna.*

He speaks so softly
that goose bumps spring up
along my arms.

Is she all right?

Baba's eyes bulge.

Now he roars.

She would have been fine
if YOU hadn't led a group of angry Muslims
to their protest.

I swallow
the saliva that's formed
like a puddle in my mouth.

Have you gone MAD, Raj?
You could have gotten yourself
and your brother killed!

        Mukhe maaf kajo, Baba.

Get inside at once.
You'd better HOPE
that your brother is safe
and comes home soon.

BETTER OFF

After what seems
like one hundred hours,
Vijay stumbles
through our courtyard gate.

Amma howls
at the sight of his slashed arm
and bruised split lip.

Mukhe maaf kajo,
I whisper in apology.

> *See what your foolishness*
> *has caused, Raj!*
> *You had no business—*

> *Neh, Baba, says Vijay.*
> *It wasn't Raj who did this.*

Amma dabs at Vijay's wounds
with antiseptic-soaked cotton,
and Baba kisses his head.

> *You were right to defend*
> *Bhavna's honor, son.*
> *She is lucky her wound wasn't deep.*

Vijay's lips curl into a snarl.

> *If that Tamir ever comes*
> *near Bhavna again, I'll . . .*

162

Baba's face turns stern.

> Under no circumstances
> do any of you leave this house.

The four of us nod.

What about the protest? I ask Vijay.
Did we stop Partition?

Vijay's eyes flash.

> Those ungrateful Muslims
> cannot LEAVE soon enough.
> Sindh is better off without them!

LONE WARRIOR

Sagar patrols our street
like a lone warrior
against unknown threats
throughout the night.

His shadow looms large
as he checks windows, doors,
making sure they're secure
while watching for thieves.

He is armed with a torch
and a long bamboo lathi stick
that he tap-tap-taps
to both annoy and warn us.

Heavy silence blankets our street,
broken only by the blast
of the shrill whistle
he wears around his neck.

I used to laugh at him,
sitting on his plastic chair,
logging details
of every vehicle that passed.

Now I'm thankful
he walks six hours a night,
staying awake and keeping watch
so the rest of us have peace.

THUMPING

When darkness falls,
a thousand fevered footsteps
rush through the streets
as people scream:

> *We've been stabbed!*
> *Our gold has been stolen!*

I press my hands
to my ears,
blocking out the sound
and dread that's building.

Though it's sweltering inside,
we don't dare open
our mangh wind-catcher shutter.
We sit in blisters and boils
from prickly heat,
my heart beating so hard
that its pulse pounds in my chest.

I want to shout:

> *Stop fighting, please!*
> *You're scaring me!*

But my words are
choked
by the thumping in
my throat.

BURLY MEN

Through a crack in the door
I spy two burly men with topis
in shalwar kameez.

I freeze, then run to Baba,
but his eyes flash with terror
and the hairs
on the back of my neck
stand up.

With the sound of thunder,
the men

BANG

BANG

BANG

against our door:

Let us in!

If you don't open up,
we'll break down this door
and slash your throats!

BROKEN KITES

In a circle, we huddle
like broken kites
before our small wooden temple
filled with mini Hindu god statues
and an agarbatti stand and bell.

Hands folded, heads bowed,
my knees shaking,
we pray to every Hindu god,
rocking back and forth,
fighting hard to breathe.

Heated shouts blend
as Sagar's lathi stick
tap-tap-taps the ground,
with his call:

Sujaag thi! Be alert!
They have axes and swords,
but I've called on friends
to help me fight them.

From the window
we see a crowd throwing rocks
at the men hurling axes
at our door.

AXE

Shouts and cries
pierce the sky
before Sagar's lathi stick
tap-tap-taps the ground,
and he calls:

Do not fear!
Our friends threw rocks
and the men ran away,
so your family is safe.

Oh, but one is running back.

He's got an axe!

He's—

CRACK.

NO MORE SOUNDS

A scream rips
through the night air
and a cold fist grips my heart.

There are no more sounds
from Sagar.
No tapping of his lathi stick.

My body won't stop trembling,
and I'm too afraid
to peep
through the crack in the wall
of our half-broken door.

All we can do
is squeeze our eyes shut
and hold each other
as our prayers echo around the room.

And it's only when the shouting fades
that we know it's safe for us,
still in our circled huddle,
to fall asleep.

LOCKS AND LATCHES

It is twenty-two days
since the
independence celebrations,
twenty-two days
since I last laughed
with Iqbal.

Because of Vijay's
wounded arm
and bruised purple lip,
Baba has made a rule
for us to stay inside with
locks and latches on.

But early one morning,
when Baba is asleep
and everything is quiet,
I watch by the window,
and before the sun rises
high enough
to stretch and yawn,
I tiptoe out.

GREEN AND WHITE

Broken pillars
and smashed windows
mark the homes I pass
as the smoky, peppery scent of gunpowder
cloaks the air.

Squares of rubble
and splattered black ash sit gaping
like the hole in my mouth
when I lose a tooth,
and I have to stop and blink a few times
at the wide hollow
where the post office used to be.

I gasp, imagining my school
that I overheard Baba say was vandalized,
and realize it might be a while
before we can go back.

Now the muezzin's voice
echoes from a nearby mosque
announcing the Adhan,
the Islamic call to prayer.

I know that Iqbal
and his family will be
standing, bowing, prostrating, and sitting
while reciting prayers in their home,
and for the first time,

when I think about him,
I feel different.

I pause before climbing the hill
to Iqbal's home,
remembering
Uncle Bari's words,

Your kind.

But soon I'm running,
my face brightening at the memory
of Iqbal and me
flying our kites.

I stop.

Hanging before me
on Iqbal's front door
is the new green-and-white
star-and-crescent
flag of Pakistan.

THEIR KIND

Now I'm surprised
to see Baba wide awake
with Uncle Mitu
and a group of their friends
marching in front of me
toward Iqbal's home
with a lit wooden torch.

Surely they know
that Iqbal and his family
will be offering namaz
and won't have the chance
to hear or see them coming . . .

My body trembles
and I want to scream,
run ahead and warn Iqbal,
his baba and ammi,
but my mind is racing
with other memories now.

Memories of the chase
by an angry group of Muslims,
    knowing what
    their kind
    would have done had they caught me
        that day of the protest,
        so now my legs and arms
            and tongue
            go still.

BITTER SMELL

Silently,
a circle of sticks and stones
is built in front of Iqbal's home
and set ablaze.

This will show them
what we're capable of
if they hurt Vijay or Bhavna again,
says Uncle Mitu.

But it wasn't Iqbal.
It was his cousin, Tamir,
I whisper as I wipe
my clammy hands
on my kurta shirt.

Flames leap and flash
with tumbling smoke.
I choke on the bitter smell
as fire rolls out across
a thick, long rope,
to the last place I expect—
the entrance of Jana's hut.

HOT RIBBONS

I scream,
NO!

Baba's eyes fly wide
when he sees me watching.

RAJ, GO HOME!

I want to run home,
run anywhere,
but my feet cannot move.

Jana kicks and butts,
eyes wild, pulling desperately
at the halter rope that binds her
to her post.

Cries come from Iqbal and his ammi
as they run back and forth in panic,
but the roaring, tumbling
hot ribbons have spread
too high and far
for their water buckets,
and his baba fumbles
with something dark and heavy.

The smoldering fire surrounds Jana
and I want to help
            but cannot move
as the blaze builds
            and my eyes water
as Jana cries out.

My chest tightens before
an explosion stops my heart—
a gunshot,
before Jana falls lifeless.

Iqbal's baba lowers his gun,
his face etched with a weight of sorrow
I've never seen before.

He wipes his tears,
and rushes with Ammi to put out the fire.
Iqbal stands very still
when the crowd moves away.

Because that's when he sees me,
and his eyes never looked
so cold.

RED TRAIL

My cheeks and lungs burn
from running
all the way home.

Words bubble
as I catch my breath,
trying hard not to hear
Jana's cries ringing loud
in my ears.

Maya pulls me to the floor,
as Nana has called
our friends and neighbors
for an urgent meeting.

With sunken eyes,
Nana draws a map of India
on the board that he's moved
from our vandalized school.

He drags a red trail of chalk
down and across the west side.

It's called the Radcliffe Line,
after the British man
who decided our future
in just five weeks.

Nana labels the left corner
and a space on the right
Pakistan,
and the middle portion *India.*

People are angry because
of where the line has been drawn.

In bold letters, Nana writes *Sindh*
on the left side of the red line.

There is a hush as my eyes dart
around the map.

> *What Nana is saying,*
> Baba starts.

But Baba cannot speak.

He covers his mouth
with both hands,
and with anguish in his eyes
shakes his head at Nana.

Nana nods
for Baba to continue.

> *Our Sindh is now*
> *part of Pakistan.*

PANIC CLIMBS

I was wrong,
mumbles Vijay as tears pool
in his eyes
and slip down his cheeks.

Sindh is majority Muslim,
so every day, more of them,
now displaced themselves,
will come to take
our homes and land.

Everyone rises
in angry commotion.
Panic climbs up my spine
and into my chest.

I am left with Maya on the floor
as a lizard scurries out
from a crack in the wall,
its gray backbone snaking,
tail flicking
before it skitters behind a faded picture.

The room reels up and down,
the earth shifts beneath me,
as I whisper to Maya
what I think I understand.

> *We are now in Pakistan,*
> *the new Muslim state.*

It isn't Muslims who will have
to leave . . .

the Kirthar hills
the Indus River
the only home we've ever known.

It's us.

HONORABLE

Amma's already packed
her kadai pot, recipe books,
mini Hindu god statues,
and the agarbatti stand and bell
and is wearing all the jewelry
she owns.

We leave tomorrow,
on a train to Bombay via Jodhpur
to stay with Baba's cousin,
Chacho Mohan,
until we can find a place
of our own.

She covers her mouth
with the corner of her dupatta,
her gold bangles jangling
as she rushes between sobs
to her room.

> *It's Nana. He's not coming,*
> says Vijay, through swollen lips.

> *What do you mean? I ask.*
> *Won't we all go together?*

> *Nana's been cremating*
> *all the unclaimed Hindu bodies*
> *since the fighting began.*

I gasp.

So that's what Nana was doing
with his bundles of branches.

My stomach twists
thinking about Nana
lifting bodies onto branches
before setting them alight
to give them safe passage
into the next life.

Vijay stands, then winces
at the pain in his arm.

>   *It's the most respectful*
>   *form of sheva,*
>   *and if he doesn't do this service,*
>   *who will?*

>   *But he'll die if he stays here!*

>   *Then at least*
>   *I will die an honorable man,*
>   says Nana
>   as he bursts through the door.

MUSTARD SEED

I know you are brave
and not afraid, Nana,
but please don't stay.

> Nana cups my chin.
> *I am afraid, Raj. Very afraid.*
> *But it's the right thing to do.*

I need you, Nana!
Mehrbani, come with us. I beg you.

Once my first tear breaks,
the rest follow
in an unbroken stream.

Slowly, Nana's expression changes
as he steps back
and folds his hands together.

> *Raj, son, have I ever*
> *asked you for anything?*

I think for a moment,
then shake my head.

> *Dear Raj, if your love for me*
> *is even only the size of a mustard seed,*
> *can I ask just one*
> *small thing from you?*

I gulp and slowly nod.

Mehrbani, don't deny
this old man the honor of serving
his country and people.
It is I who beg you for your
permission and blessing.

Nana bows, his eyes glistening,
and I fall to my knees.

Nana holds me tight,
his arms saying what his lips do not,
that he loves me,
that he's proud of me,
and that now, I must be brave.

WHOLE WORLD

Before leaving
I fetch the sack
that Amma gave me
to pack
my whole world into,
two kurta shirts and suthan pants,
a deck of cards,
a spinning top, my toothbrush,
and Nana's small Indian flag.

My kite waves in the doorway,
as if to say goodbye.

Its blue wheel takes me back
to charging through the fields with Iqbal,
cool breeze on our cheeks,
suthan pants flapping,
our feet barely touching
the ground.

Iqbal always loved my kite.
Iqbal also loved Jana.

I swallow hard, staring down
at the scarred knuckles
of my hands
that did nothing
to save her
as her cries fill my head
like they do each night.

I know it would be
                foolish
                        dangerous
                                and just plain stupid
                                        to go . . .

SLINGSHOT

I creep under
Iqbal's back window,
my cricket bat and kite
gripped tight.

Suddenly, a rock flies at me
and I duck just in time
to see Iqbal's eyes flash fire
as he pulls back another rock
and aims his slingshot
straight at me.

Get out of here!

I duck again as my hands fly up
in surrender.

> *We're leaving today, Iqbal.*
> *I just came to say goodbye.*

He vanishes
and reappears
by the pile of rubble
that was once a wall.

His face seems older,
with a purple bruise around his eye.

GOODBYE

Slowly, I rise.

I'm giving you my kite, I say,
offering it with one hand.

                    I don't want it.

Look, I just want to say . . .

                    What?

About the fire—

                    You were THERE!
                    And you did nothing
                    to save Jana.

I lower my head.

I wanted to.

                    KURO! he screams,
                    charging into me
                    like a head-bent bull.
                    My bat and I
                    crash to the ground.

I'm not lying, Iqbal! I wanted to!

                    Then why didn't you?

We wrestle in the dirt,
slapping and kicking
at ribs and shins
till he pins me down
and presses a knife
against my neck.

I was scared! I scream.
*My family was angry
after Tamir hurt Vijay and Bhavna.*

> *We are not all like Tamir.*
> *My parents and I*
> *didn't hurt anyone.*

I know that, Iqbal.
That's why I joined the protest
instead of flying in the Kite Festival.
I thought it was you who had to leave.

Iqbal's eyes narrow.

> *Your brother was foolish*
> *to protest with guns and knives*
> *without telling us.*

He sighs, pulls the knife away,
and slowly rises to his feet.

> *You gave up the chance*
> *to be named King of Kites*
> *for me?*

I shrug and nod,
standing up to brush away dirt,
ignoring the stings
from the scrapes on my skin.

I've cried every night for Jana,
and I promise I'll find a way
to make it right.

Iqbal's eyes search mine.

Mehrbani, I say, offering my kite,
with two hands this time.

He steps forward and snatches it.
Then he walks two steps away
and stops once more.

I hold my breath, praying
he won't reach for his blade again.
Slowly, Iqbal turns,
and before I can move,
he stumbles forward and pulls me
into a tight embrace.

> *I wish it could be*
> *another way*, he whispers.

TOPI

Are you going to leave
without this?
Iqbal asks, offering me
his topi for protection.

What he wants to ask is,
Are you going to forget me?

        Never, I whisper,
        holding out my hands.

He looks at his topi,
then into my eyes.

I'm trusting you with my topi,
along with my pride
and honor, he says,
gently placing it on my head.

        Vari garjandasi, Iqbal,
        we'll meet again,
        I say with a bow.

Lifting his palm to his face,
fingertips to his forehead,
he bows in return.

Till then, may God
be your guardian, Raj.
Khuda hafiz.

He hands me my cricket bat,
nods with a smile,
and, holding my kite,
walks away.

PARCELS

I step
from shadow   to   shadow
most of the way,
then speed up
as I round the corner to the station,
leaping over
discarded parcels,
my sack slung over one shoulder,
my bat gripped tight in the other hand,
when a pack of boys running up the lane
overtakes and surrounds me.

Their leader arrives,
his arm in a sling,
and my lips start to quiver
when I see that it's Tamir.

Quickly, I hide my face
behind my sack.

What did I say about
staying in pairs
so you don't end up like one of them?
he says, pointing to the parcels.

I look again and see
instead of parcels, bodies.

Something cold ripples up my spine.

Slowly, I nod and walk on,
one trembling step before the other,

when Tamir shouts,

Wait!

Sweat beads gather on my lip
as I stare down at the ground,
close my eyes,
and suck in my breath.

In one swift movement,
Tamir lunges before me
and adjusts the topi on my head
with his bat.

That's better, he says.
Then he raises his bat to the sky
and charges ahead.

WEIGHED DOWN

Small colonies of hawkers
have sprouted
around the station,
selling betel leaves, tea,
and cigarettes.

I have never known the station
to be so busy.

I stare at Amma's friends,
all weighed down with worry.

*Why is Aunty Sundri's back
bent like that?* I ask Vijay,
who holds tight to Maya's hand.

>   *From the weight
>   of the family diamonds
>   stitched into her petticoat.
>   It's the safest place to put them.*

*And Aunty Neelam?
She never swayed
like that before.*

>   *She's hiding
>   her neighbors' children
>   under her sari folds.*

*But why are they hiding?
Where are their parents?*

Vijay shakes his head sadly.

Those children
don't have train tickets.
If they're caught, they'll be shot,
but if they stay, like their parents,
they'll die anyway.

STILL MOMENT

I think about the British man
who came for the first time
to draw his line
and wonder why
I never thought it would lead
to . . .

      the
           long
                line
                      that
                          we're
                              joining
                                  now—

                                                to board the train.

In this line, Baba and Amma
bid farewell
to Uncle Mitu, Aunty Neelam,
Aunty Sundri, and friends of families
they've known for generations.

Holding each other's arms,
they hear the words
their lips do not speak
as shoulder squeezes,
hair ruffles, and forehead kisses
shower Maya, whose face is red
and wet with tears.

Vijay embraces Bhavna,
his bruised lips
kissing the wound on her head.
He clasps hands with Dhruv and Sham,
clenching his jaw
so his tears won't fall.

Baba stares one last time
at the only land
he has ever called home.

Slowly, he bends,
touches his fingers to the earth,
then to his head for a small, still moment
before rising again,
and when he's not looking,
I do the same.

ABANDONED

Dust swirls like fireflies
as we approach the train
with heavy bags
and heavier hearts.

Two bags only!
the station guard spits.

Baba's lips
press tight together.

He grabs Amma's bag
and I want to shout,
Mehrbani, Baba,
she needs those things,
but my words are stuck
as he pushes past the crowds
and dumps it
among other abandoned bags
in the dirt.

> *Ne kar!* Amma calls
> after her recipe books, saris,
> and black-and-white memories.

> Baba's nostrils flare
> as he shouts, *Would you have me dump*
> *our money, clothes,*
> *and silverware instead?*

I can hardly see the train
with all the people
draped over it.

Some squat on haunches
on its roof,
some hang by their arms
from windows.

CRAMMED

We are greeted
by searching eyes
in the crammed carriages
that promise to carry us safely
to our new home
in Bombay.

Home.

Can such a word
be used
for another place?

People smile with tight lips,
and it's no coincidence
that everyone is dressed in white,
the color we wear
when someone dies.

STUCK

I ache for Baba to give me
a job to do, so I can show him
I am brave,
      strong, and
            capable like Vijay,

and he'll finally say,

Dado sutho. Very good.

When Baba speaks,
his voice is stern,
like we're studying a math sum
I can't afford to get wrong.

Vijay and Amma will watch the bags.
I'll take care of our tickets and papers.
Raj, watch Maya.

I roll my eyes,
wishing Maya was a lizard
and would just disappear
so I wasn't always stuck
with her.

Through a cracked window
I take one last peek
at the home I am so scared to leave,
yet more terrified
to stay in.

I fill my lungs to the fullest,
trying to save the sweet air
to carry with me,
but all I can breathe is heavy dust
and the smell of sweaty bodies.

HOLDING ON

I squat
between Vijay and Maya.

Where are we going?
she asks for the third time.

        To India, Vijay says, irritated.

But we're already in India.

        Not anymore.
        Somebody changed the rules.

The driver blows a long blast
of the whistle.

Crows caw in the chikoo tree
as the carriage rolls forward
and scenes of our homeland
flash faster and faster.

The *clickety-clack*
makes my eyelids droop.

It is twenty-four days
since the independence celebrations.
I wrap my arms around my knees,
holding on for as long as I can
to the warmth of Nana's eyes,
the joy of Iqbal's laughter,
and my whole world:
Sindh.

RED BUCKET

I'm hungry, Raj,
Maya whispers.

> Eat your share of the koki
> that Amma packed.

I already finished it.

> Then take mine.

I already finished yours too.

My stomach grumbles
for my piece of thick flatbread
with onion, green chilies,
pomegranate, and coriander.

I'm thirsty, Raj,
Maya whispers.

> Drink a sip of water,
> but only one sip every few hours.

Sleep crawls over me,
and as I sink into slumber,
Maya taps my shoulder.

I need to go, Raj.

> Use the red bucket in the corner.

That bucket smells, Raj.

Will you come with me?

I groan.

Okay, Maya, let's go.

And under my breath
I whisper,
I wish you were a lizard.

CONNECTED

I've lost count
of the days and nights,
listening to the rumbling of empty stomachs,
wheezing of windpipes,
whispers, rumors
about terrible things happening
in other towns.

The train comes
to a screeching stop,
and metal scrapes against metal
as dark shapes slump all around me.

The air is foul
as if sweat from unwashed bodies
and urine have been
sprayed like perfume.

I hear other sounds, whispers
from the train next to ours, from people—
traveling to their new homes
in Sindh.

Shadows flash in a scattered dance
against the train walls.
I scoop up my sack and tiptoe past
a snoring Vijay
and drooling Maya
to the cracked window.

From the station lights
I see fathers, mothers,

and children
all dressed the same as
Iqbal, his baba, and his ammi,
clutching tight to all they have,
the weariness in their faces
heavy with pain,
just like us.

Even if all the Hindus
in the world stop liking
all the Muslims in the world,
I never will.

GREEN EYES

I freeze
at the sight of a boy
watching me watch him,
his eyes green as the lime
that swims in Baba's limo pani.

He is younger than me,
wearing the same topi as Iqbal's,
which is squashed inside my sack.

With a finger to my lips
I reach for Iqbal's topi
and smooth it out with care
before I place it on my head.

The boy's eyes widen,
his mouth falls open.

I send him a wink.

He tries very hard,
but with all his effort
he can only blink
the same way I did
before Iqbal taught me how.
He blinks and blinks
and I try not to laugh.

When he finally manages a wink,
I wave goodbye, tucking Iqbal's topi
back in my sack
before settling back down,

hoping sleep will carry me
the rest of the journey.

I wonder if the boy with green eyes
    will run in my courtyard,
        climb up my mango tree,
            sleep in my bed,
                and I also wonder
                    if the new kite,
                        green fields, and great big bungalow
                            that will all soon be mine
                                when we reach Bombay
                                    actually belong to him.

BLACK BEETLES

Vijay shakes me awake.

It is early morning
when we arrive in Bombay.

My lips are parched,
my stomach hollow,
and I am still rubbing the sleep
from my eyes when
Baba cries,

Chor! Stop, thief!

Words fly
between Baba, Vijay,
and the big, beefy man whose eyes
glint like black beetles
alongside his
shaggy-haired sidekick.

It takes me a few seconds
to realize that they're grabbing
our bag of money, clothes,
and silverware.

I reach for my cricket bat.

Daggers flash as fists smash faces.
I raise my bat,
willing myself to strike
the shaggy-haired man

clean across his chin so that
he'll drop our bag.

But when my arms swing back
and the bat rises high in the air,
my hands tremble, my eyes water,
and I freeze.

I stand like a statue,
sweat drenching my skin,
ringing screams vibrating in my ears,
and a pounding in my chest
as Baba is kicked, Vijay is punched,
and the thieves escape with
our treasured items.

SAFE SIDE

I lower my bat as people scramble
and push past me,
shoving and elbowing
each other like animals
in their haste
to get off this train.

We are finally on the side
of the border
where they told us
we belonged.

The safe side.

Relief washes over me.
We can now live without fear
of being hated or hurt again.

Slowly, Baba reaches
for the one bag
that Amma has guarded with her life
as Vijay shrugs
and Baba shakes his head,
muttering under his breath,

All he had to do was swing the—

Then the only sound
is Amma's shrill scream:

       Raj, where's Maya?

PART V: CRASHING

PROMISE

For two long days
and nights
we search for Maya,
rushing past crowds at the station,
offering my bat
and the shirts on our backs
for information.

Baba refuses to stop
for a wash and rest
at his cousin
Chacho Mohan's home,
only accepting his salty
onion pakoras and water
with the same promise
each day:

When we find Maya,
we will come.

DUSTY CASES

We search all day
and at night
slump next to strangers
against the rails with dusty cases
and crumpled papers.

We wait and pray
that Maya will come back to us
as waves of shame
ripple through me.

I feel sick for wishing
that Maya was a lizard
and would just disappear.

Amma turns her head
so I cannot see the tears in her eyes,
cannot hear her
weeping with the fear
of not knowing
where her daughter has gone.

Baba turns his head
so I cannot see his disappointment.
His silence says everything
his lips do not.
He is angry and ashamed,
and instead of Maya disappearing,
I think he wishes
that it had been me.

BABA'S WRATH

Amma hands me
an onion pakora.

I'm not hungry.

But Amma knows
the grumble of my belly.

>   *Raj, you need to eat something.*

Baba's veins pulse
in his temples.

>   *Why are you fussing over him?*
>   *We should be searching for—*

>   *We are searching for her.*
>   *Raj still needs to eat.*

>   *Why does HE need to eat?*
>   *When his sister is out there*
>   *lost and starving because of*
>   *HIM?*

Baba strides toward me,
takes me by the arms,
and releases his wrath by
shake
            shake
                        shaking me.

He stops,
turns away to pace,
rubbing the back of his neck
as he whimpers,

My little girl. My chikoo.

He takes
my shoulders
and shakes me again.

I quake as his
red face in mine
roars,

*All you had to do
was WATCH HER!*

Then he shoves me
to the ground.

I curl into a ball
and sob.

SHOEBOX

It is three days
since we've come to Bombay,
and Chacho Mohan visits again.

This time,
our hearts and bellies
are so empty,
we take one last look around
for Maya
and follow him to his car.

We drive through town,
where everything
is fast and loud,
cars honking,
traffic lights flashing.
I try my best to spot her
among the buildings that loom high above,
some as high as ten floors.

On the sidewalks,
I search among the people
with towering baskets of bananas
on their heads
as they weave between
smart-suited men in turbans
with long beards,
carrying even longer umbrellas.

The streets heave
with red double-decker buses,
and even there, I look for her

as men swerve between them
on rickety bicycles.

When we arrive
at Chacho Mohan's home
on Nepean Sea Road,
it's not at all what I expected.

Though he says it's
opulent for Bombay standards,
it's crowded
with overstuffed
sofas and rickety end tables.
Like a shoebox,
compared to our bungalow
in Sindh.

THIN, STRAIGHT LINES

Chacho Mohan appears
just as he did
in his photographs—
potbellied
with slicked-back hair
and a bushy black mustache.

Baba says he's supplied
the British with high-end pottery
and achieved great success.

Chachi Geeta stands tall
next to him,
with a pointed nose and chin,
and on her wrist
four gold bangles
jangle louder than Amma's.

Her face is the same
as her nine-year-old twin daughters,
Asha and Beena,
pale as milk, lifeless eyes,
all three mouths set
in thin, straight lines.

*Asha and Beena are so happy
to give up their beds
for you and Keshav.
They will sleep on the mats
in the living room
next to Vijay and Raj,*
says Chachi Geeta.

Amma says I am lucky
to have cousins to play with,
but I know better.

I can see beyond
their twisted smiles.

After Vijay sneaks out,
I hear them whispering
on their mats
about how unlucky
their poor cousin Maya is
to be somewhere out there,
scared and alone,
all because her silly brother
couldn't do as he was told.

CHEMBUR CAMP

We leave early for the
Chembur Camp in Trombay.

It's a converted military barracks,
says Chacho Mohan,

a place for refugees
who have nowhere else to go,
and you might find Maya there.

We wander the halls
with their crumbling ceilings
and musty dampness,
searching behind
the hundreds of flapping curtains
made of torn gunnysacks,
which act as walls.

We find
sobbing women,
        hungry children,
                and violent clashes
                between men from
                Punjab and Sindh.

                Maya is nowhere.

Though I really want to find her,
I am glad she is not here.

I can see the earthworms
and scorpions that live

in the running water,
along with human feces
that flows from broken pipes.

The worst is the latrine,
one for twenty families.

There's a broken door,
an open drain
with mosquitoes and rats everywhere.
I only go when I cannot
put it off any longer.
My eyes burn from the stench,
and I can't help but vomit a little after.

We search for Maya all day
and hang our heads as we leave
the camp, each of us sickened
by the sights and smells,
and that's when I see it.

Squashed into the earth,
trampled and muddy,
is a small flag of India,
all its colors faded.

I try to remember
Nana's words from a day
that seems so far away.

The colors of the flag
and the colors of our people

aren't simply
saffron, white, and green,
but courage, faith, and peace.

A lump forms in my throat.
Just like the rulers of
Britain, India, and Pakistan,
who failed us
when they drew that line,
I have failed Nana
when I showed no courage on the train
and lost my faith at the station.

My eyes squeeze tight,
my breath ragged
as the strength leaves my legs
and I fall to my knees.

Tears course down my cheeks
and a moan escapes me.
I know now
        that Maya
                isn't ever coming home.

                Wherever that is.

TEMPLE

Where is your home temple?
Amma asks Chachi Geeta
as she holds up her bundle
filled with mini Hindu god statues
and the agarbatti stand and bell,
covering her head,
ready to pray.

> *We don't have a temple*
> *but a prayer cupboard in our bedroom.*
> *You are welcome*
> *to come inside and pray*
> *whenever you like.*

Oh, may I come now?
I've just had a bath
and before I eat,
I'd like to pray.

> Chachi Geeta hesitates.

> *Right now*
> *I'm in the middle of something.*
> *Perhaps later today?*
> she says, shutting her door.

DOORBELL

Each day
when the doorbell rings,
I spring up
and fly to the door,
hoping that it might be Maya,
who has somehow found us.

I try not to care
that Chachi Geeta,
Asha, and Beena snicker each time,
and I soon grow used to the voices
of the washerwoman, sweeper,
and milk wallah.

Sometimes I pretend
it really is Maya.

That we do a happy dance
and after that,
I never forget
to watch her again.

But day after day,
it's never Maya,
and before I know it,
I stop glancing up
when the doorbell rings.

LETTER

A letter arrives for Vijay.

From the way
        his face comes alive
at the sight of it
        and how his smile
spreads across his lips
        as he reads it,
everyone knows
        it's from Bhavna.

Be sure to ask
after her parents and Dhruv,
says Amma, handing him
a piece of foldable blue gummed paper
called an aerogram, along with a pen.

Vijay folds the letter carefully
and places it in his pocket.

He thanks Amma for the aerogram,
but instead
of sitting down to write
as we all expect him to,
he places the gummed paper and pen
neatly by his sleeping mat
and walks away.

GROWL

Mehrbani, Amma,
may I go downstairs
to the communal garden?

Mehrbani, can I have a few paisa
so I can find a kite seller
and maybe buy a new—

> *You will NOT leave this house,*
> Baba growls,
> *or even dream of flying a kite.*
> *Not when your sister is still*
> *out there . . .*

He chokes on his words
and takes a breath to calm himself.

Then Baba's eyebrows furrow.

You always asked to help
in the kitchen.
Now you will stay by
your mother's side
and chop and grind,
all day long.

GOD'S TEARS

It is twenty days
since we've come to Bombay.

In Sindh we desperately prayed
for rain,
but not one kind drop fell.

Nana said that rain brought
new life,
      cleansing,
            renewal,
                  and always good fortune.

Yet here
the rain spills down like God's tears
every day,
      flashing
      pounding
      sheets
drowning out
      all other sounds:
      whining Asha,
      squealing Beena,
      howling Chachi Geeta.

Even without the rain
at least in Sindh we had a community.
People laughed, cried, and ate together.
If we were there,
each of them would be searching
for Maya.

Here, no one even
speaks Sindhi.
We live in cramped quarters
above and below
people whose family trees
we do not know.

I wish I could tell Nana
that the rain doesn't bring
all those things he said.
        The rain, like God's tears,
        only helps wash away
our tears
        before
                anyone
can see them.

UNTOUCHED

A third letter
arrives for Vijay.

Again his face
comes alive.
Again a smile
spreads across his lips.

But the aerogram by
his sleeping mat
remains untouched.

Bombay walls
are thin enough
for me to hear the whispers
between Vijay and Amma.

Don't you miss her?

        Of course I do.
        You wouldn't understand . . .

But I understand.

I understand that a blue aerogram
just like my kite
with its wheel of blue
was born to fly.

And if Vijay
isn't going to launch it . . .

AEROGRAM

I decide
to write to Nana.

Talking to him
always makes me feel better,
        and if I tell him
        that I miss him,
        maybe he'll come join us,
                or at least he'll write back
                to let me know
                he's still alive.

The one thing
I must not tell him
is that I lost Maya.

It would break his heart
to know that she is missing
because of me.

It would break my heart
to know he's disappointed
because of me.

I think I'll tell Nana
about the boy with green eyes
instead.

DEAR NANA,

I wish I could stroll
by your side along the Indus.
That we could plop our feet
in the crystal waters
and watch the pallo swim.

Here, there's nothing to watch
except the pouring rain
falling all day and night.
Someone must have heard
your prayers.

Here, there are no kites to fly,
no trees to climb,
no mangoes to pick,
no markets to visit,
no Iqbal to play with.

Here, there are only nasty men
who took our bag on the train,
our money, our clothes,
our silverware,
and other things too.

I hope you are safe
and will write back
to tell me that you're coming soon,
because that would make
everything better.

And if you see a boy with green eyes
who just moved to Sindh,
please tell him that the boy on the train
who taught him how to wink
is your grandson.

ALL IT TAKES

It is forty-five days
since we've come to Bombay.
Forty-five days
since I lost Maya.

I stare at the rain for hours,
wondering if somewhere out there
Maya is staring
at the very same rain
and if she's afraid like me.

Every part of me is desperate
to get out, do something,
go to school even,
so that I can make a friend,
but I'm not allowed to register
until Baba finds work.

Baba wears
his ajrak shawl
and his father's lucky watch.

He and Vijay
go from shop to shop,
hoping someone will place
an order for a salwar suit design
that Baba clutches
in his faded green folder
with the red elastic band.

Before they leave
each morning,

Baba lectures Vijay,
It's about creating a demand
for what you want to sell.

When they return
every evening
with no orders,
Baba lectures Vijay again.

All it takes is one
happy customer
for news to spread.

PERFECTION

Chacho Mohan offers
Baba work
in one of his pottery stores,
but Baba's lips twist,
and in a quiet voice he says,
I will make it on my own.

Here, no one
scurries around him
with a lemon-water finger bowl.
There is no freshly pressed jacket
or lunch tiffin for him to take
with nowhere to go.

When Vijay isn't visiting shops
in search of work,
he sleeps through the day,
sometimes mumbling
Bhavna's name
before sneaking out each night,
and I wonder where he goes.

Amma and I help Chachi Geeta
prepare meals and roll papads,
since they only have one cook.
Their gold bangles
tinkle together
as they pound herbs and spices,
making beautiful melodies
and fragrance.

I am secretly thrilled
to be allowed in the kitchen
and do my best to
grind
    stir
        and roll
spices, curries, and phulko
to perfection.

CRACKLE

At first Chachi Geeta
is happy to have our company.
Amma hardly ever smiles
except at the crackle of cumin
and the sweet fragrance
of tamarind chutney.

Then one day ...

Oh! groans Chacho Mohan.
*This spinach and lentil curry
is just delicious!*

Chachi Geeta and Amma
exchange a look.

The spices! The flavors!
Chacho Mohan takes another helping
and licks his lips.
*Geeta, this is the best sai bhaji
I've ever tasted.*

Chachi Geeta's
forehead wrinkles.

> *I didn't make
> the sai bhaji today,* she says.

*Oh, it was Neha?
Well, I think you might
have to take lessons from Neha, then!*
he says with a chuckle.

BATTLE

Behind their bedroom door
Chachi Geeta and Chacho Mohan
are at war.

How dare you suggest that I
need lessons from HER?

I was only saying . . .

It's hard enough to share
our home, our food,
and have our girls sleep
on the floor!

Calm down, Geeta,
they will hear.

So let them hear!
They should know they've overstayed
and need to find
a place of their own
before I go mad.

They have no money
and nowhere to go,
so please be patient.
Imagine if it were us.

Well, it's not us!
And I don't want her
in my kitchen anymore!

But Neha's food is so—

Mohan!

Okay, fine, but at least
for her peace,
when you're not at home,
let her have
that corner in the kitchen
that you don't use.

SHADOWS

It is sixty-four days
since we've come to Bombay.

With nothing left to do,
slowly, Amma loses her voice,
and by evening her eyes
have faded into pools as dark
as monsoon rain.

Like her, I desperately miss
the chopping, kneading,
and chatter of the kitchen.
It gave us an excuse to be together,
blending herbs and spices,
making magic.

Baba's gold ring and gold chain,
Amma's earrings and bangles,
have been sold to pay for food,
but who will pay the cost
of their broken hearts?

Their clothes are as faded and frayed
as their blank stares out the window,
with a thin veil
that's gray and cold
like the rain.

Cold and numb, they stand
broken and empty,
shadows of the people
they used to be.

PART VI: RISING

NANA'S PROMISE

After days of watching Amma
fade like a falling kite,
I remember Nana's words,

Hold on tight.
Soon the wind
will change in your favor,
just as long as you
don't let go.

Without my kite,
all I have to hold on to
is Nana's promise.

An idea comes to me.

Waking earlier than the sound
of Chachi Geeta's shuffling champals,
I plead with Amma to teach me
how to make her sweet
mango pickle.

But why? she asks
as we tiptoe to the kitchen.

                    You'll see.

Every morning for a week,
she teaches me how to
measure out the spices,
chop the raw mango,

and test the sugar syrup
with her special touch.

Sweet mango pickle
was Maya's favorite.
Making it together
is special.

Like magic,
Amma's smile returns,
and when Chachi Geeta
is out running errands,
I secretly deliver the pickle jars
to other families in our building
as gifts to them,
so neither Amma nor Chachi Geeta
will ever know.

TROUBLE

Three days later
our doorbell rings.

It is a man named Gani
from the second floor,
who I call Uncle out of respect.
His eyes dart around the room
and his brows knit together.

*Tell me at once
who sent this jar of mango pickle
to my home!*

My mouth goes dry.

> *Pickle? Why would
> anyone send . . . ,*
> Chachi Geeta starts.

Asha and Beena
point fingers at me.

> *Raj?* Amma asks.
> *Did you do this?*

So, it was you, was it?
Uncle Gani asks.

I bite my lip.

Baba frowns, takes me
by the arm.

Raj! Apologize at once
for causing this trouble!

A little titter
ripples through the room,
followed by spluttering laughter.

Yes, young man,
you've caused me
a great deal of trouble.

He holds his belly
as his eyes shine.

Because now
I can't enjoy my meals
without your mango pickle!

PICKLE

From that day Amma receives
daily orders from families
in the building
for every kind of pickle,
from carrot to lime to green chili.

Baba says nothing
about Amma's success.
I catch him peeking inside the kitchen
when he thinks
no one is watching.

Chacho Mohan claps his hands,
but Chachi Geeta wears the face
of someone who has swallowed
too many spoonfuls
of castor oil.

After three weeks,
Amma is selling
jars of homemade pickle
for one rupee each,
and Baba is confused.

I still don't understand
how you came up
with such an idea, Raj.

He pours his hot chai
from teacup to saucer
before lifting it to his lips.

Well, Baba,
it's about creating a demand
for what you want to sell.

I swallow my smile
when Baba spills his tea
and then stares,
like he's seeing me
for the very first time.

You see, all it takes—
I wink at Vijay—
is one happy customer
for news to spread!

MIRACLE

It is one hundred days
since we've come to Bombay.

I know this because every morning,
after I sit cross-legged,
close my eyes,
and ask the Hindu gods,
especially our Sindhi god Jhulelal,
who is known for riding
on a brave pallo and granting miracles,
to keep Maya safe
and help her find us,
I draw a little line
on the wall next to my bed,
so I can remember
all the promises I have
to believe in.

At least the lines I draw
        don't
            hurt
                people.

                      And today, even the line of
                        Amma's big, wide smile
                          extends into mine.

I visited Principal Shaw
this morning, she chirps,
sounding like she might just
sprout wings and take off.

He liked my mango pickle so much
that he placed a regular order
and . . . Oh, Raj, tomorrow
you're going to school!

UNIFORM

I am light and bouncy
as a kite.
Excitement leaps
all the way up my arms
as Baba returns
with my brand-new
blue-and-white-striped uniform.

Without a word,
he hands it to me.
I lock the bedroom door
to try it on.

The fabric is stiff
and scratchy on my skin,
not soft like
the cotton-rich kurta tops
that Baba made.

The armholes pinch,
the collar pulls tight around my neck,
the pants sag,
even when I adjust the inner band
to the last button.

I gaze in the mirror
and smooth out
my new clothes.

For a moment, the memories
of running carefree
with my kite in the wind

as Maya chased after me,
tugging at the bottom of my kurta top,
come flooding back.
I have to blink
these thoughts away,
before tears prick my eyes.

I never needed a uniform in Sindh.

Now I'm bouncing
from foot to foot with excitement,
eager to dress
like all the other boys
and somehow feel
I belong.

WAITING

On my walk to school
there are
no green fields,
no mango trees,
no Indus River to toss stones into.

Instead, the air is heavy
with busy people
rushing across dusty streets
and swerving cars that beep
for no reason.

It might be just like
your school in Sindh,
says Amma, adjusting the collar
of my tight, stiff shirt.

I frown, remembering
Masterji's wooden stick,
and hope I won't be made to
squat and rise up
again and again
when I fail a math test.

Then my spirits lift, knowing
it will still be worth it,
for the modern classrooms,
large playgrounds, and friendly faces
all waiting for me.

LOST KITE

In this city school
we sit along benches,
not cross-legged on the floor,
like we did in Sindh.

I raise my hand
to answer questions
so that everyone will know
I'm smart
and want to be my friend.

I even raise my hand
in math.

By the end of lesson four,
I notice that the only one
raising their hand
for kind, gray-eyed
Miss Jhaveri
is me.

We're glad to have you, Raj,
she says at the end of class.
I'm sure our boys and girls
will make you feel welcome.

Miss Jhaveri's smile
is like a cup
of Jana's warm and soothing
rose-scented milk,
but she's the only one
smiling.

The others send me curious
sideways glances.
At break time, they huddle
in hushed whispers.

At lunchtime,
they thunder in swarms
around the field,
boys kicking balls,
girls chasing one another,
their spiraling laughter mocking me.
I drift like a lost kite
to the side of the field,
alone.

NIRMAL

On my third day,
King of the Field,
broad-shouldered Nirmal,
with hair short and spiked
and a gang of friends behind him,
taps my shoulder.

Is it true that you're
from Pakistan?

>   *No, I'm from Sindh.*

They burst into laughter.

Nirmal smirks and mutters,
New boy doesn't even know
where he's from!

SACK OF SAND

My classmates babble
in languages
I cannot understand.
Marathi,
      Gujarati,
            and Punjabi,
depending on which corner
of India
they're from.
The language I am forced to use
to make myself understood
is English,
which is funny, because I thought
we were free from British rule.

When writing in Hindi,
I can't control the pencil
for the twists and turns needed
to form the *ha*,
the sharp edges of the *ra*,
and the tight curls of the *cha*.

By my fifth day, I feel the strain
like a sack of sand
on my shoulders.

Sitting at the end of the wooden bench,
I run my hands through my hair.

After trying once again
to read
from left to right

when I have always read
from right to left,
    I sigh, my index finger lingering
    beneath every word,
    hoping to squeeze meaning
    out of each symbol,
        when all I really want to do
        is read, write, and speak
        in the language of my heart,
            but along with my home,
            my language
            has been taken away.

GRAY EYES

I throw down my book
with a thud.

Miss Jhaveri glances up.

Her kind gray eyes meet mine.

Please pick up that book, Raj.
Kiss it and touch it to your head.
We respect knowledge
in this classroom.

The room is silent
as thirty pairs of eyes
burn holes into my head
and I wish the ground would
open up
and swallow me.

Then Nirmal whispers,

> *New boy, meet me at the field*
> *at lunchtime.*

I'm not sure what he wants,
but since he's the only one
who speaks to me,
I'm going.

THE FIELD

When I reach the field,
where a long pole with the Indian flag
flies high,
a group of fifteen
have gathered in a semicircle,
as if waiting
to watch a show.

Mr. Doshi, who is bald,
apart from the few strands of hair
that he strokes across his head,
is on lunch duty.

He waves to us
before Nirmal's friend, Varun,
whispers something in Mr. Doshi's ear
that makes him hurry back
into the school building.

Nirmal, a true king,
stands center stage
and waves out to me.

I walk onto the muddy grass,
goose bumps rising along my arms,
and stand next to Nirmal.

Friends, let's welcome Raj today,
our new friend from Sindh.

I feel a flush of happiness
as hands clap in applause

and whistles fly, welcoming
ME!

It's not at all what I expected,
and a warmth I haven't felt
in the longest time
spills inside my chest.

You only have to do
one small thing, Sindhi boy,
to join our gang.

I hesitate.
Is this a trick?

Varun, who's wearing a smile,
stands on my other side,
and together they jump into the air.

It's simple, Raj.
Just jump a little higher than us
and you're in!

They crouch down
and spring up high into the air,
then give me
the thumbs-up sign.

Then the crowd starts to chant,
Jump
  jump
    jump
      jump.

I lick my lips,
focus all my energy
on squatting as low as I can go
and springing up high.

CRASH!

I'm on the ground,
blinded by spots of flashing color
and a crushing pain
around my skull.

When I jumped,
Nirmal and Varun
kicked my feet forward,
sending my head smacking hard
to the ground.

My eyes squeeze shut,
willing the pain
and mocking laughter
to stop.

Nirmal holds his sides,
howling loudest,
before they all run off
and he calls behind him,

Welcome to the club,
firangi!

FIRANGI

My head still throbs
when I reach home,
the ringing in my ears so loud,
with the word *firangi*.

Why would he call me *foreigner*,
the word we used for the British?

Aren't we all
Hindu and Sikh brothers,
living on the
"right" side of the border?

Aren't we all on the
same side
                    now?

There's no time to ask.
Amma has orders to prepare.

If Maya were here,
she'd be the one helping Amma
in the kitchen,
giggling away,
her bed of curls bouncing
in swirls on her shoulders
as she chatted on endlessly.
Now her chatter and giggles
are someplace far away,
and there's only one person
to blame.

I drop my bag and rush
to fry the okra
and chop green chilies,
to make five batches
of kadhi curry,
stealing a few bites of the thick,
sweet flatbread mithi loli
as I do.

To complement the kadhi,
Amma prepares the
besan-flour sweet boondi
and crispy fried aloo tuk
as I inhale the
scent of home.

We've had four orders for
spicy pallo as well!

Amma holds her chin
a little higher
and has expanded her corner
of the kitchen—
the side that Chachi Geeta
doesn't use.

She sees me
clutching the back of my head
and her eyes soften.

What happened, Raj?
You're quiet today.

       It's nothing, Amma. I'm fine.

I tell Amma that her kadhi curry
is tangy, with just enough spice,
but I'm also trying
to tell her,

You make wonderful food
and deserve our respect
for being the gentle breeze
that carries us.

Her brown tin box of money
is filling up
with more notes than coins,
and I'm so happy
to see her smiling again,
I don't have the heart
to tell her about
what happened at school.

NO ONE ASKS

Baba and Vijay return
and my jaw tightens
when they complain
about their long day
of walking the streets.

They can't seem to
see us
still working hard
after our long days.

No one asks
        how my day was.
No one asks
        anyone anything.

Vijay has dark rings
beneath his sunken eyes
from sneaking out each night.

I want to ask him where he goes
and if one day, I can go with him,
but I remember
what I did at the protest
and then again on the train,
so I don't ask him anything at all.

Baba gives Amma
more work
by asking her to make chai for him.

I busy myself
making flavorful fish gravy,
browning onions
in ginger and green chilies,
adding tomatoes, turmeric,
and chili powder,
then coriander and cumin powders,
and a pinch of garam masala,
stirring quickly
before leaving it to bubble
on a low flame.

Then I prepare the cumin rice,
green chutney,
and kachumber salad
while Amma cleans the fish.

Amma and I know
that the pallo in Bombay
isn't the same,
can never be the same
as the fragrant, mouth-watering
pallo from Sindh,
but we do our best.

LEATHER CHAMPALS

Nirmal is waiting for me
at the school gate
when I arrive.

I try really hard to meet his eyes,
show him I'm not upset,
but the closer I get
the more the knot in my stomach
twists tight,
and I have to turn away.

Morning, firangi!

I force a smile,
but my lips feel stiff and dry
like leather champals
left too long in the sun.

*Look, no hard feelings,
it's just what we call
your kind.*

Your kind.

His words land
like a punch to my gut.

Nirmal pats me on the back,
walks me through the corridor
as he clasps hands
with floppy-haired Varun.

But now you're one of us.
Well, almost . . .

I stop.

You just have to do
one more thing.

I shake my head,
turn to walk away,
when Varun grabs my shoulder.

His eyes are pleading.

> *Come on, Raj,*
> *I want you there.*

My eyes dart
from Nirmal to Varun
and my lips twitch,
wanting to demand that first,
Nirmal stop calling
me a firangi.

But instead,
I say nothing.

Varun gives me
a slap on the back.

> *See you at the field*
> *at lunchtime.*

COWARDS

It is 107 days
since we've come to Bombay.

Mr. Doshi is on field duty again.
He is eating
one of the cheese and chutney
sandwiches
he usually smells of.

There are only three boys
on the field
when I reach them.

Nirmal, Varun, and Jasvinder,
a Sikh boy who arrived
from Punjab two weeks before me,
who's skinny and wears spectacles
and a blue patka around his head.

Ah, Raj, just in time—
meet Jasvinder.
His family were cowards too,
running away instead of fighting
for their homeland.

                    I . . . we . . . didn't run.

Well, you didn't stay, did you?
Or you wouldn't be here.

Varun darts to Mr. Doshi
and whispers in his ear.

Mr. Doshi pauses, shrugs,
and walks back into school.

He believed you?

                              Not at first,
                              but I said it was urgent.

Great job, Varun.
Raj, come help us
answer Jasvinder's question.

Jasvinder cocks his head
to one side and twists
the metal kara around his wrist.

Varun takes Jasvinder's arm.

Raj, hold his other arm.

Nirmal's eyes narrow,
and when he makes a fist,
my knees wobble.

                    What was Jasvinder's question?

I take Jasvinder's other arm,
holding tight,
hoping I'm not going to end
up on the ground again.

He asked if I would stop
calling him a firangi.

Before I can blink,
Nirmal's fist flies hard
into Jasvinder's stomach.
He crumples to the ground,
sobbing as hard
as my hammering heart.

Now he has his answer.

ALWAYS A SEAT

Nirmal and his friends
are nice to me after that.

There is always a seat
at their table,
always space on their soccer team
for me to play,
always a clasp of my hand,
a slap on my back,
a funny exchange,
especially with Varun,
who licks his lips
at my tiffin of spicy lentils.

And all I have to do
when Nirmal picks
on another new boy who moves here
is hold my breath
and look away.

TENSION

Chachi Geeta and Amma
stand in the kitchen
back-to-back.

Chachi Geeta is pounding turmeric,
       chili powder,
              ground coriander,
                     ground cumin,
                           ground ginger,
                               and pepper
                               to make curry powder.
Amma is grinding cinnamon,
       peppercorns,
              cardamom,
                     mustard seeds,
                           coriander seeds,
                           cloves,
                           and nutmeg
                           to make garam masala.

Chachi Geeta's bangles crash,
creating a cacophony of
screeches
       and squawks
              like birds
                    that were once set free
                        but have been shot down.

FLOWERS

Asha and Beena
sit at the table
making flowers
out of colored paper,
scissors, tape, and sticks.

Look at mine! sings Asha,
holding up a pink one.

> *No*, shouts Beena,
> waving a purple one,
> *look at mine!*

They stand up
to show them off,
but then their flowers droop,
the petals coming unstuck from Asha's,
the leaves flying off Beena's,
and all that's left
is a mess on the floor.

Asha's eyes water,
Beena's nose leaks,
and they both start to wail.

I bend down to pick up
every petal and leaf,
then sit down and reach
for fresh paper
and some new sticks.

Asha's and Beena's heads tilt,
eyes blink, and
they stop sniffling
and come sit next to me.

> *Ready to try again?*
> I ask.

PAPER GARDEN

I try to remember
how Maya and I
made paper flowers.

My mouth is dry
with missing
as my hands wrap green paper
around a stick,
cut baby zigzags into leaves,
fold and refold paper,
yellow, purple, pink,
and sketch the outlines of petals
before cutting, curling,
layering, and gluing each one
to make a blooming
paper garden.

Asha and Beena squeal
and clap their hands.

I didn't like you before,
but I do now, says Asha,
handing me a blue flower.

> *I like you too,*
> says Beena, giving me
> an orange one.

> *Thank you for these,*
> *but what I'd really like,*
> I say with a grin,
> *is the leftover paper.*

RULES

At break time
when Varun and I are alone
I ask the question.

Why is Nirmal so mean?
Especially to anyone new?

Varun flips his hair
and it flops back over
his eye.

> *After Partition, Nirmal's father*
> *lost his job and home*
> *to a man from Sindh.*

My jaw drops.

> *That's why Nirmal doesn't like Sindhis*
> *and calls you cowards*
> *for leaving your homes.*

Do you think I'm a coward?

Varun shrugs.

> *It doesn't matter what I think, Raj.*
> *I'm not King of the Field.*
> *Nirmal hates anyone new*
> *because he wants to be the only king.*

He made three rules
to protect himself.

Rule number 1:
Everyone listens to Nirmal.

Rule number 2:
Anyone new must pass a test
to join his gang.

Rule number 3:
If Nirmal doesn't like you,
nobody likes you.

JUST ANOTHER SOUND

It is 116 days
since we've come to Bombay.

Sometimes I pretend
to stare out the window,
for a long, long time,
but what I'm really doing
is trying to remember the sound
of Maya's voice.

Night walls
are still too thin,
and though my pillow in Sindh
was thick, the paper-thin chaddar that
wraps around me
on my straw sleeping mat
doesn't block out noise
the same way.

We should give the money
you've earned
to Mohan and Geeta
as some form of rent!
shouts Baba.

> *We need to save it, Keshav,*
> *so we can move out of here*
> *and rent a place of our own!*
> yells Amma.

Baba and Amma think
we cannot hear them

blame one another for the money,
clothes, and silverware
we lost,
the gold-stitched tapestries
we forgot to bring.

When Amma starts to cry
and Baba smashes
another whiskey glass,
I know they're
thinking about Maya.

I lie awake,
staring at the dark, starless sky,
trying to believe
that Amma's cries of heartache
are just another night sound
like the buzzing of cicada bugs
and the sheets of rain
battering the window.

Vijay has snuck out again,
the frame of his shape
on his sleeping mat
formed by bulked-up pillows.
I wonder what he's up to
and where he goes,
but mostly I worry,
what if he doesn't come back?

PROJECT

Asha, Beena, and I
sit at the table
with paper, markers, tape, string,
scissors, and sticks.

They cut, fold, and create
star-shaped lanterns
while I work
on a secret project.

I draw the blue wheel
that welcomes change
on a white piece of paper,
flip it over, tape it to a vertical stick,
tape a shorter horizontal stick a quarter of the way down,
fold the sides over, cut away the excess paper,
and tape the sides down.

Is that a pirate ship?
asks Asha.

                Or a fighter plane?
                asks Beena.

I cut some string to tie to each side
of the horizontal stick,
attach the ball of string to the loop,
fold and cut tissue paper into thick strips,
and tape them to the base.

We give up, Raj.
What is it? cries Asha.

Please tell us,
pleads Beena.

I lift my masterpiece
high into the air
and grin.

It's a lion, of course.

SOUR TASTE

Nirmal is waiting again
as I reach the school gate,
and my gut churns.

Good news, Raj!

He pats me on the back.

There's a new firangi in school,
and I'm giving you the chance
to be King of the Field.

You know what you have to do.

A sour taste fills my mouth.

I shake my head.

           I don't think I can—

You're doing it, lunchtime
tomorrow.

CENTER STAGE

When I reach the field,
the same group of fifteen is gathered
just like before in a semicircle,
and soon I'm standing
center stage.

I clear my voice, scan the crowds.
My neck burns hot,
and sweat trickles like a snake
down my back.

Where is Mr. Doshi?
Isn't he meant to be on lunch duty?
I ask Varun.

> *I poured a spoonful of laxative*
> *into his chai this morning.*
> *No one has seen him since!*

I struggle to breathe
and through shallow gasps
send a silent apology
to every boy
for what I'm about to do.

Because deep down
I know
I'll never be the silver pallo
that's strong enough to swim
against the current.

Friends, I begin.
Let's welcome . . . um.
Let's, um . . .

Nirmal walks out
and stands firm
next to me, taking over.

                              Friends, we have
                              a new student today.

Once again, hands clap in applause
and whistles fly as I watch
to see which boy is going
to crack his skull.

But walking slowly onto the field,
a bed of curls swirling, like Maya's,
isn't a boy at all.

It's a girl.

FLYING AGAINST

My throat tightens
and my heart

drops

into my stomach.

Welcome to our new
Sindhi friend, Anju!
shouts Nirmal, who explains
that all she must do to join our gang
is jump a little higher
than him and me.

Then he signals, and we both
squat down and jump up.

She hesitates
and tilts her head.

> *I'm not sure*
> *I want to jump,*
> she says.

All the air gathered up
in my chest
sighs out of me.

It's simple, look! says Nirmal,
who nods as we duck down
and jump high again.

She turns to me, and I see
that she is skinny
with a button nose, a dimpled chin,
and an eyebrow raised
to the sky.

Is it simple?

Her brown eyes are trusting,
so much like Maya's
that I cannot speak.

I can only hear the gentle
voice of Nana,

*Did you know
that a kite rises highest
when it flies against the wind?*

Raj, jump! shouts Nirmal.

My teeth clamp tight
before
we crouch low
and shoot high into the air,
then Nirmal gives her
the thumbs-up sign.

The crowd starts to chant
even louder than they did with me,
Jump
   jump
      jump
         jump.

We squat low, she leaps high,
and as Nirmal kicks her foot forward,
she starts to fall and . . .

I catch her.

PART VII: SOARING

HERO

At first no one speaks.

Then slowly, whispers bubble
across the semicircle,
growing louder
in a rapid chorus questioning
what just happened.

Nirmal starts to clap.

Well, well, what a hero you are,
Mighty King Raj!

He nods to Varun,
who hesitates, mouths, *Sorry,*
then starts clapping,
and soon the whole semicircle cheers
with false applause.

You could have joined us, Anju,
been welcomed into the flock,
even though you cowards
don't deserve it,
but now . . .

He shoves me hard,
      shoves me again.
           I try to stand my ground
                but someone else shoves me
                    from behind

and I trip,

falling flat

in the mud.

Nirmal sniggers.

Raj has ruined
any chance you had.

FINDING A FRIEND

After Nirmal leaves,
I stand up, wipe the grime
off my face and pants,
take in a breath,
and sigh, my heart still
battering inside.

Why did you do that?
Anju asks.

My cheeks flush.

        I . . . I don't know.

I start to walk away.

Did they . . . do that to you?

I stop, turn around,
and stare at the grass.

Then I look at her
and nod.

She chews on a fingernail
as my hands fidget
with the hem of my shirt.

Well . . . , she says,
*I was ready to fall
and crack my head
if it meant I might find a friend.*

Her words
make my eyes
grow wide.

Don't be sad, Raj.
You don't need Nirmal.
Now you've got me.

You coming?
She steps forward
and twists my nose,
just like Iqbal used to,
before running back to class.

STRONG

Miss Jhaveri's
kind gray eyes
see everything.

The dirt in my hair,
      the grime on my pants,
            my shaking hands.

She scans the room,
catching stolen looks
at Nirmal, Varun, and me,
and solves
the equation.

I wonder who can tell me
what makes a strong person?
she asks.

           Someone with muscles!
           says Varun, flexing his.

The class bursts into laughter.

I'm afraid not.

           Being a leader,
           says Nirmal, sitting smug.

That's not correct either.

All eyes are on Miss Jhaveri.

A strong person
is someone who stands up
for themselves.

Eyes from every corner of the room
dart toward me.

And do you know
who the strongest people are?

> *Who?*
> asks the class in
> unison.

The strongest people
are those who stand up
for others.

GIRL FROM SINDH

After school,
I wait by the gate
for the girl from Sindh
I know nothing about,
but who already makes me feel
like fitting in
might not be so important
after all.

I grin when Anju says
she only lives a street
away from me.

We walk together
and she talks about
her home in Larkana,
which is north of Hyderabad
but still close enough
for her to play in the same
Indus River as I did.

Throwing sticks,
        tossing stones,
                diving deep for silver pallo
                in the cool refreshing water
                that I miss so much
                it hurts.

She tells me about her best friend,
Noor, who is Muslim.
They had to share
their sweets in secret.

I say nothing because the things
I have to say are just too big.

A lump of joy
forms in my throat,
because now I have someone
                    to walk with,
                    to talk with,
                            someone who knows
                                where I've been,
                                what I've lost.

TORTURE

The next day,
when Principal Shaw is in a meeting,
Mr. Doshi isn't watching,
and Miss Jhaveri's nose is in a book,
each member of Nirmal's gang
targets me in the hallways.

Aarav
shoves me,
    Simran
    kicks my shin,
        Jiya
        trips me up,
            and Deepak
            punches me in the gut.

The only one who meets
my eye is Varun,
but his lips stay shut.

WHAT WE LOST

When Nirmal's gang
goes off to the field,
Anju and the other new kids
who have each had a taste
of Nirmal's medicine
huddle in a small corner
of the playground.

*I'm sorry that I helped them
hold you down,* I say to Jasvinder.
I didn't know that Nirmal would—

    *After what you did for Anju,
    all is forgiven,* he says with a nod.

Four of us
sit in a circle,
sharing
      our food
           our stories
                our hearts
and speak of the homes
we had to say goodbye to.

Anju tells us that her family
traveled to Karachi
and came by boat,
squashed together like fish in a tin,
and the waves caused waves
                inside her.
She could hardly walk
after five days of throwing up.

If it wasn't for a kind lady
who fed me crackers,
I think I might have died.

My nani, who was too frail
to join us,
stitched a doll for me, Devi,
to always remember her by.
I lost Devi on the boat,
but I hope that one day,
I'll find her again.

Jasvinder describes
what happened to him
on the way to the train.

My family had to lie down
on the ground
and pretend to be dead
as a group of men
stole our money, clothes,
even the three boiled sweets
from my pocket.

Zia starts to cry.

She shares about
her journal of thoughts that
she had written in since
the age of nine.

It was a book of all my memories.
I lost it on the train,

and I know I'll never get it back,
because the pages were needed
for cleaning backsides.

Everyone is silent after this,
and I hope nobody asks
if I lost anything,
but Anju's eyes search mine,
her head tilting to the side.

It wasn't something I lost.
It was someone.

They lean closer to listen.

I lost . . .

I lower my gaze.

I lost my grandfather, Nana,
who chose to stay behind in Sindh.
I lost my best friend Iqbal too.

I don't say anything else.

FRIENDS

The blended scent
of saffron and cardamom
fills the air
as Amma prepares to slice
her freshly rolled varo.

With careful force
she cuts across the center,
and I lick my lips,
imagining the sweet crunch
of pistachios, almonds,
cashew nuts, and poppy seeds
with hardened caramel.

All at once, the varo
shatters into fragments,
broken slivers
flying in different directions,
their edges left in crumbled dust.

Amma's shoulders slump.
She lets out a sigh
and shakes her head.

It's okay, Amma, I say,
pushing the broken pieces
together again.

> *You're in a good mood,*
> she says.

The corners of my mouth lift.

I made some friends today.
Anju, Jasvinder, and Zia.
They've all moved, like me.

> *That's wonderful, Raj.*
> Amma puts down the knife
> and wipes her hands
> before embracing me.

Over her shoulder
I see Baba standing in the doorway,
his eyes misted over
with a faraway look.

> *Having friends can help*
> *the fractures in your life*
> *heal faster,* he says.

> He walks toward us,
> scoops up a handful
> of the broken varo pieces,
> and tosses them into his
> mouth.

> *And life tastes sweeter too.*

LENTILS

It is 120 days
since we've come to Bombay.

I ask Amma to make
an extra tiffin
of dal chawal
for my friends at school.
Then I laugh
as Anju, Jasvinder, and Zia
moan with pleasure on the playground,
gobbling every grain of
the flavored lentils.

This is too good!
says Anju,
licking her fingers.

Your amma
should open a restaurant!

I tell her
Amma has started delivering
to families who place large orders.
I'm helping her
drop off some food today.

Anju replies with
the very last thing
I expect her to say.

Can I come?

HANDSHAKE

On our way to Amma,
Anju teaches me
a special handshake
just for us.

Forehand slap
       backhand slap
              double click
                    hands clasp together
                         pull back and point.

We try it a few times,
then stroll on,
and I can't stop smiling.

FAMILIAR

Amma beams
at the sight of Anju,
and tears shine in her eyes
when Anju helps
pack up her boxes of food.

At first, I think
it's because she's happy
I've finally found
a friend in Bombay.

But the more Anju
chatters and laughs
and her bed of curls
bounces in swirls on her shoulders,
I realize
that's not the reason.

REFUGEE

Each family we deliver food to
shares a different story
about how they left
Sindh,
Punjab,
Delhi,
Bengal.

Some by train, others by ship,
some by bullock cart
and then on foot,
walking for days
in the deathly heat,
all with different stories
about
who got sick,
      who got robbed,
           who got hurt,
              and how many
              family members they lost
              along the way.

The person I want
to listen to most is Aunty Jyoti,
whose husband, Uncle Murli,
died only a few months ago.

When I taste your mother's
mutton pulao—ooh!
It's like I'm home again.

Aunty Jyoti is sixty-five,
with silver hair.
She is frail and walks
with a limp.

It's from the chill I caught
in that Kalyan Camp in Ulhasnagar.
Fourteen of us shared a mattress,
and it was always wet.

My face crumples
when I imagine life in the refugee camp,
where it stank
and disease spread
from having only one lota vessel
for drinking, washing your body,
and cleaning your backside,
and where so many families
still lived.

> *I'm glad you left, Aunty,*
> says Anju, patting her arm.

It wasn't easy, Aunty says.
My Murli only made money
when he let go of his dream
to sell jewelry,
like he always did
back in Sindh,
and started trading shoes.

I think of Baba and Vijay,
walking the streets each day
searching for tailoring work.

I don't know what broke
my Murli's heart more.
Losing everything the first time,
or forcing himself to forget
the memories, like a passing season,
so he could move on.

As she speaks,
I wonder if maybe
it might be time for
Baba to move on too.

LASTING SWEETNESS

We sit in silence
in Aunty Jyoti's kitchen
as Amma peels and cuts
a sweet, ripe mango.

Take a piece.
Mangoes are meant
for sharing.

The soft, juicy flesh
tingles on my tongue
and, for a moment, takes me back
to clambering up tree trunks
with Iqbal.

Perching at the top
with our golden treasures,
the tangy, thick juice
exploded in our mouths
before we nibbled and gnawed
at the precious seeds,
sucking our prizes till our lips
were left with rings of orange.

That was good.

So, so good.

I don't think
I can ever eat another
mango in my life, Iqbal.

Me neither, I'm stuffed.

Same time tomorrow?

My eyes squeeze tight,
flooded with scents, textures,
and flashes of the past.

HEALING HEARTS

As Aunty Jyoti waves goodbye,
she thanks Amma
for doing so much more
than just cooking
and delivering food.

You're healing people,
she says, her eyes glistening.

> *Aunty Jyoti really enjoyed*
> *your mutton,* says Anju.

> *The food takes her back*
> *to everything she lost,*
> says Amma.

> *You take her back,* I
> say.

The line
of my mouth stretches
from ear to ear,
because for the first time
in a long time,
my heart feels full.

When we drop Anju home
and meet her parents,
we do our special handshake,
then quickly,
before I change my mind,
I grab her nose and twist it.

I link arms with Amma,
who seems different somehow.
Now she stands a little taller
and her smile reaches
all the way up to her eyes
like she's come to life.

We march together,
singing all the way home
and into the hallway,
where Baba stands with
his arms crossed.

ERUPTION

THAT'S IT!

Baba shouts.

        What is it? Amma asks.

Baba paces
up and down
as the lava inside him
bursts out.

It's all your cooking
and delivering,
keeping you so busy all day long
that you're never here to
make my chai!

Amma and I exchange a look
as Chacho Mohan leads
Chachi Geeta,
their faces filled with concern,
to their room.

You must stop this foolishness!
We will soon find serious work
so you can just stay home
and cook for us.

Amma's eyes fill with tears
as all the joy
of our afternoon
drains out of her.

BUBBLE RISING

Amma hangs her head
and turns to walk away,
but a small bubble of lava
deep inside me rises
and I say,

NO!

Vijay turns in surprise
as Chacho Mohan, Chachi Geeta,
Asha, and Beena
peep out of their room.

Amma's business isn't silly.
She does more than
just feed people.

What are you talking about?

She heals hearts.
The hearts of people
who lost their homes like us.
And she's the only one
making money, so—

RAJ! Baba roars.

Everyone loves Amma's cooking, I roar back.
You can't find a tailoring job,
so maybe it's time
you let go
and try something new.

318

Baba's eyes bulge with rage.
His nostrils flare,
and he marches toward me,
raising his hand.
I brace myself
for the slap that's coming.

Then he stops.

Amma, Vijay, and I watch
as without a word
he stomps off
to Asha and Beena's room
and slams the door.

VIJAY'S SECRET

That night,
when Vijay sneaks
out of the house,
I follow him.

Stopping and squatting
in alleyways
as he crosses streets
and runs through lanes,
I only just manage to keep up.

He stops
at Cooperage Bandstand Garden,
where ponies trot,
hot roasted nuts are sold in paper cones,
and a Ferris wheel spins, its light
throwing shadows all around.

Vijay moves with care
toward a set of trees,
trees that beckon like old friends,
and once again
I fly up, silent and nimble
as a squirrel.

From way up high
past the big green coconuts
surrounding me,
I see Vijay meet three mustached men,
who are older, potbellied,
and none of them
are smiling.

Did you bring the loot?

        Did you bring my sister?

I clasp a hand
over my mouth
to stop
my scream.

BROWN TIN BOX

First show us the money,
then you'll get your sister,
says one of the men.

Vijay pauses,
then reaches inside his satchel
and pulls out a brown tin box.
Amma's tin,
holding all the rupee notes
she's earned from cooking
since we've come to Bombay.

A bitter taste fills my mouth.
It would break Amma's heart
to learn that he took it,
but Amma would be so happy
to see Maya again.
I know if I was Vijay,
I would do the same.

Open the tin.

        First, my sister.

If we don't see the money . . .

        Okay, see, it's all here.

Vijay fumbles with the tin
filled to the brim with notes,
along with a big piece
of my mother's heart.

Hand it over.

Vijay looks quickly
from left to right.

       Where is my sister?

I squint to
catch sight of her
bright brown eyes, cheeky grin,
and deep brown curls that swirl
on her shoulders . . .

but no one's there.

YOU SAID

All at once
the three mustached men
pull knives.

Hand it over, boy,
and we might not
hurt you, says the leader.

          You . . . you said you had my sister.

          Vijay tries to sound calm,
          but the crack in his voice
          betrays him.

My body tenses
and I'm back on the train
with men shouting,
knives flashing,
my sweaty palms
holding tight to a cricket bat
that refuses to swing.

          You said you had Maya!
          Vijay says again, unable to stop
          his voice from rising.

We just told you
what you wanted to hear, says the man,
swiping the tin filled with notes
and raising his knife to
Vijay's neck.

LIME-GREEN COCONUTS

As the three men pounce,
my hands work quickly,
and
one
              by
                        one
just how Iqbal taught me,
the big, heavy, lime-green coconuts
fly down
on each of their heads.

Far heavier
and more deadly
than any mango seed,
the great big coconuts rain down

THUD

CRASH

CRACK

and Vijay takes off
into the darkness.

ALLEYWAY

When I catch up with Vijay,
he is crouched in an alleyway
against the wall, shaking,
as gut-wrenching sobs
tear through him.

He sees me and stands up
as his cheeks flush.

You followed me?
That was foolish, Raj.

> *Who do you think*
> *threw the coconuts?*

SWEET DREAM

Vijay stares at me in disbelief.
His eyebrows shoot up, and he laughs.

Then we talk,
really talk, about how
empty and angry
he's felt
since we all lost Maya.

I never blamed you, Raj,
not once.
I blamed myself.
I'm the oldest and had to fix it.

His voice shakes.

I had to find Maya
before I could allow myself
to write to Bhavna.

As Vijay takes a deep, pained breath,
I wonder if my brother has been
too independent
and has more to forgive
than just the British.

I walked the streets
night after night,
asking if anyone had seen her,
till I met these men.

They said it would cost me,
so I promised them money
I didn't have.

Then at night, I heard
Baba and Amma fighting over
what to do with her money,
so I thought that
if I took it—

                    We'd find Maya
                    and they'd stop fighting,

I finish his sentence,
my eyes brimming with tears
from the sweetness
of such a dream.

RELIEF

Vijay and I sneak in
at four thirty in the morning
to find everyone waiting.

Asha and Beena woke
       Chachi Geeta, who woke
              Chacho Mohan, who woke
                    Amma and Baba,
                            to tell them we were missing.

What were you thinking?

Baba asks,
the deepest lines etched into his face,
making him look
one hundred years old.

After Vijay explains
about the men
and the money
and the knives,
Baba doesn't roar
like he usually does.

He sits down in silence between us
and gently places
his trembling hands
onto each of our backs
as tears slip slowly
down his face.

Amma stands still as a statue
in the hallway
and Vijay rushes to fall at her feet,
saying he is sorry,
that he'll help her
make back all the money,
every last rupee.

But she cannot speak,
only shakes her head,
pulling both of us
into her embrace.

LADOOS

I have an idea.

Amma, since we have hours
before Anju fetches me for school,
and since your food always
makes everyone feel better,
can we please make ladoos?

Even though we only eat
the sweet balls of flour,
sugar, ghee, and cardamoms
on special occasions,
sweet ladoos with salty tears
might just be exactly what we need.

Amma's eyes lower to the floor.

    I'm not sure that's such a good—

        That's the best idea I've heard all week,
        says Chachi Geeta, wiping her face.

Amma stands frozen
as Chachi Geeta
takes her by the hand
and leads her to the kitchen.
Asha and Beena
happily skip in after them.

        I'll sift the besan, says Vijay,
        who rolls up his sleeves
        and drapes his arm over my

shoulder
in a way he hasn't done
since forever.

Amma takes out
a heavy-bottomed pan,
then waits,
stealing a glance at Baba,
who blinks back tears
as he quietly stands
beside us
and reaches for a wooden spoon.

SHINING BRIGHT

Vijay sifts the besan,
Amma and Chachi Geeta
grind the sugar and cardamoms,
then add the besan and ghee
and roast the cashews
before Baba and Chacho Mohan
take turns
stir
        stir
                stirring
the mixture.

Can I stop now?
asks Chacho Mohan.

        My arm is getting tired,
        complains Baba.

          Keep stirring,
          commands Chachi Geeta
          as she adds the extra ghee.

            And do not stop until
            the mixture turns golden brown,
            orders Amma, lifting the pan
            off the stove.

Asha, Beena, and I
hold our sides, giggling
at the big, strong men in our family.
Then my fingers dance
and I tickle my cousins

just the way Nana did
with Iqbal and me.

When the mixture has cooled,
we take small portions
and roll them into balls.

*How are your ladoos
so shiny and perfectly shaped?*
Chachi Geeta asks Amma.

*That's one of Neha's
kitchen secrets,* says Baba,
with a hint of pride.

*But there are no secrets
between family,* says Amma,
showing Chachi Geeta
how she rolls her ladoos
in a muslin cloth for a
smooth finish.

And the smile
Chachi Geeta sends Amma
shines brighter
than all the ladoos
on the counter.

JOINING IN

When Anju walks in,
every one of us
is joking and singing,
our hands and elbows,
faces and chins, all smeared
in ghee, sugar, and besan flour.

Anju takes one look at us
and joins in.

She giggles and chatters,
taking baby bites
from the ladoo she's shaping,
and both Baba's and Vijay's
eyes sparkle
just watching her.

NOOR

Anju usually walks to school
jibber-jabbering,
but when I tell her about Maya,
she's quiet.

I remind them of your sister,
don't I?

                  I stop walking, turn to Anju,
                  and nod.

You're going to find her,
you know.

I shrug.

                  What if we don't?

Then she'll live
where Noor lives.

                  Where's that?

Anju smiles.

In here, she says,
patting her heart.

We walk on
and I wonder what to say
to make Anju
as happy as she makes me.

Tell me about Noor.

Anju's eyes light up
as she describes shared mischief
with her frizzy-haired,
hazel-eyed friend,
pinching sweet chikoos
from the market,
inking secret henna
messages on their palms,
and cheating in games
of kabaddi.

> *We cheated too!*
> I say, remembering Iqbal.

We keep walking,
each remembering,
swallowing
hard.

BABA'S PLAN

Baba has a serious talk
with Chacho Mohan.

Whatever you need, Keshav,
you have my support.

Chacho Mohan has a serious talk
with Chachi Geeta.

If Neha's food business
can turn a profit
in just a few days,
I've agreed to give them a loan.

A loan for what?

For them to rent
their own home.

Chachi Geeta is silent.

I've started to enjoy
having them around.
But I'll help in any way I can.

By the end
of all their serious talks,
Chachi Geeta has a smile
across her face as bright as Diwali,
and Baba and Chacho Mohan
shake hands.

Baba straps on his lucky watch
and asks if I'll stay home
for the next three days,
because he has a plan.

SWEET SAMPLES

In the morning,
Asha, Beena, and I chop
almonds and pistachios
to garnish portions
of Amma's sweet,
golden seyun vermicelli,
which she and Chachi Geeta
roast to perfection
in ghee, cardamom, and saffron,
while Baba, Chacho Mohan, and Vijay
fry the seasoned potato chunks.

In the afternoon,
I go along with Baba,
Chacho Mohan, and Vijay
from store to store,
handing out
sweet samples and flyers
that list all of Amma's dishes.

You know, son,
Baba says, with a hand
on my shoulder,
I got this idea from you!

In the evening,
Asha, Beena, and I soak, fry,
and stir all the ingredients
needed for orders
that have started to come in,
and Anju rushes over
after school to help too.

MOTHER

Amma is humming
the Bengali song we sang
to celebrate the
motherland's freedom
at independence.

We have each pinched off
a chunk of dough,
pressed them down in atta flour,
and are rolling them out
into flat circles,
side by side.

*Nana taught us this song
to celebrate Mother India,
who wasn't going to be told
what to do anymore, right?*

She was set free.

Amma nods as silent tears
spill down her cheeks,
and now I feel bad for saying
something wrong,
wondering if she's crying
because she misses
Maya and Nana and Sindh
or because Mother India
wasn't set free
in the way we'd all hoped.

Then her arm reaches around me,
she kisses my cheek,
and she whispers,

>*Thank you, son.*

For what, Amma?

>*My independence.*

SECOND DEAL

Mehrbani, Raj, can you help me
prepare the masala pallo?

I glance up, amazed
that Vijay is asking
for my help.

> *Isn't Baba helping you?*

He shrugs.

Baba has a hot temper
when ours doesn't come out
as good as yours.

I turn to him.

> *I'll help you,*
> *and then let's tell Baba*
> *how we help each other.*

Why?

My eyes dance toward
my special project
by the door.

> *If we can be honest with Baba,*
> *I'll help you with the pallo*
> *and show you something special.*
> *Deal?*

Vijay's eyes light up,
his fist clasps mine,
and my heart bursts.

Deal.

LOOSEN YOUR LINE

Early in the park
Vijay and I fly paper kites
in the Bombay sky.

I can hardly feel
where my hands end
and the reel begins
as our kites climb and fall,
fluttering without care
about formulas and shapes,
our laughter rising to meet them.

When my lion flies wild,
I hold on tight.

Vijay watches and, like me,
holds tight
to his kite string.

But when the force is too strong,
sometimes the best thing to do
is loosen your line for a while.

Vijay follows
as I let out my line,
and our kites rise high with the extra slack,
almost gliding on their own.

> *I have much to learn from you,*
> *little brother,* says Vijay,
> slapping my back.

*I thought I knew everything
about flying,
but you might just have
a better way.*

The wind ruffles our hair
and kisses our cheeks,
as we look up together,
grinning wide
at our tumbling kites.

BLUE GUMMED PAPER

I'm ready to write to Bhavna,
says Vijay.

But where is my aerogram?

Amma and Vijay
hunt under sleeping mats,
then search my face
with raised brows.

> *Sorry, I took it,*
> says Asha.

> *No, I took it,*
> *sorry,* says Beena.

My cousins wink at me.

> *It doesn't matter*
> *who took it,* says Chachi Geeta.
> *Because I have one more for you.*
> She hands the blue gummed
> paper to Vijay.
> *And an extra one for you too,*
> she says, handing an aerogram
> to me.

When no one is looking,
she winks at me too.

EARNED

By the fourth day
Amma receives so many orders
that I have to stay home again.

Baba double-checks
the great stack of order sheets.

He bows his head
and folds his hands in prayer
by the window.
Then he wipes his eyes
and turns to me.

Raj, do you remember
when I told you
that your dada wasn't just a tailor,
that he had a special instinct for business
and that's how he earned
this lucky watch?

He carefully hands me
the Rolex Oyster watch
with the white and brown dial,
square silver base,
and Roman numerals for hour markers
that his father left him.

There were many things
your dada tried to teach me
that I couldn't learn
until you showed me.

I stare at the watch
in my open palm as my jaw drops,
and Baba places his hand
over mine.

You have the same instinct
as Dada,
and you bring us the same luck
as my father's watch,
so now this belongs to you,
because, son, you've earned it.

ANJU'S WISH

Amma asks Anju
if she can help prepare
twenty tubs of
mint coriander chutney.

*I'll pay you
for the extra help.*

Anju is quiet.
Then the corners
of her mouth turn up
and her eyes sparkle.

> *All I really want
> is to take your food
> to the kind old lady who helped me
> four months ago on the boat.*

That's a sweet thought,
says Amma.

*Of course we'll take her some food.
Do you know where she lives?*

Anju bites her lip and nods.

> *She said she was going
> to the Kalyan Camp in Ulhasnagar.*

Baba, Amma, Vijay, and I
share a look.

The very last place
any of us ever want to go
is to another refugee camp
after what we saw
and all that Aunty Jyoti shared.

> *Your food helps take them back,*
> Anju says in a small voice.

And her eyes are so pleading
that Amma replies,
If your parents agree,
then yes, we can make a trip.

> And even Baba says,
> *You're not going to that place*
> *without me.*

OURS

By the fifth day,
Amma, Baba, and Vijay
can manage the orders,
and Baba has good news.

I made a deal with Chacho Mohan,
he says with joy expanding
across his face.

Now that we've raised
a good sum of money
with your mother's food business,
he's agreed to give us a loan
to rent our own home!

Vijay punches his fist to the sky.
Amma smiles all the way
up to her shining eyes.

I am soaring,
        flipping,
                spinning with delight inside.

Our own place.
        Our own space.
                Just ours.

PART VIII:
TOUCHING THE SKY

LINES THAT MAKE YOU SMILE

It is 127 days
since we've come to Bombay.

Anju and I
do our special handshake.
Then she skips and twirls
as we hand out our ladoos
to Principal Shaw, Mr. Doshi,
and a beaming Miss Jhaveri
and share them at lunchtime
with Jasvinder and Zia.

Before we know it
       a large group of kids
             are forming a line
                   behind floppy-haired Varun
                to ask if
                    they can have one.

My eyes narrow
and I fold my arms
across my chest.

They're the same kids
who pushed me
and tripped me up.
Why should I share
my ladoos with them?

               Just imagine Nirmal's face
               when he sees all his friends

queuing up to eat your ladoos,
Anju says, raising an eyebrow.

I grin,
holding out my box
of sweet balls to share.

POWDERED GLASS

Everyone loves
our ladoos so much,
especially the kids
in Nirmal's gang.

Don't eat those firangi's sweets!
Nirmal shouts at Varun,
who tries his best
to hide
his munching.

Now there's a fire
in Nirmal's eyes.

When he opens his mouth,
his words, like a sharp manjha
coated with the powdered glass,
fly out,
ready to cut me down.

Payback's coming.

LION AND LAMB

After school
Nirmal circles me,
      stalking me
      on the playground,
            eyes daring me
                to meet them.

Before, I would have
looked down
      looked away
            looked anywhere
               but at
               those piercing eyes.

Now I look back.

We're fighting
right now, Raj,
you and me.

                No, Nirmal.

Let's go to the field
and finish this.

                I'm not coming.

Come on, you coward,
fight me like a man.

I will not
fight you, Nirmal.

You'll fight me,
because if you don't . . .

He steps forward
and whispers something in my ear
that makes the ladoos in my belly
curdle.

My fists, teeth,
and body clench tight.

Let's go.

IF I WIN

We watch
as Varun whispers
to a boy named Jai,
who holds his stomach
and runs to Mr. Doshi,
saying he's going to be sick
from eating too many ladoos.

Mr. Doshi has no choice
but to quickly guide him
into the building.

I shift my weight
from foot to foot,
my eyes fixed
on the saffron, white, and green flag
that flies above our school.

Let's do this! shouts Nirmal.

If I win this fight, he says,
*and you're down on the ground
for more than three seconds,
you'll stop sharing your dirty food
and only speak
to the other firangis
from now on.*

> *And if I win, then
> I become King of the Field.*

For a second, Nirmal's eyes grow round,
then he smirks and nods.

Your name might be Raj,
but you'll never be king.

Before I can reply,
         he throws the first punch
and kicks me in the stomach,
         knocking the breath from me.

Then he sends another punch.

         Now I'm

         down
         on
         the

         ground.

COLORS

STOP! What are you doing?
shouts Anju.

Why are you fighting?

> *Anju, I have to,*
> I say, picking myself up
> off the ground
> and raising my fists.

But why?

> > *Get her out of my way!*
> > says Nirmal.

> *Anju, leave!*
> I shout.

Not till you leave!

I'm so busy
watching her,
I don't see the
next
      punch
         coming

and I'm back

    down

    on
    the
    ground

with my head throbbing
and a shooting pain in my gut
so sharp
I cannot move
as the colors of
saffron, white, and green
spin like a pinwheel
above my head
until darkness closes in.

RED

A blurry vision
of Nirmal appears.
I blink a few times
as he shoves someone backward,
calling out,

ONE . . .

He shoves again,
throwing them off-balance,
then turns around to smirk,
and I realize he's pushing
Anju.

> *No!*
> But it's too late.

TWO . . .

Nirmal is
white-knuckled with gritted teeth.

I told you, Raj,
> *that if you don't fight me,*
I'll fight Anju.

A knot forms in my stomach
and everything
slows down
as he pulls back his hand
to send her a slap . . .

And I'm on my feet,
seeing

red.

ENEMY KITES

I charge into Nirmal,
shoving him hard,
and he tumbles to the ground.

He springs back up
and takes a swing.
I slip to the left.
He lunges forward
and bashes me in the gut.

I'm going to break you in half, Raj.

I catch my breath.

We circle each other
like enemy kites
soaring and swooping
in the sky.

> *You can't fix yourself*
> *by breaking someone else,* I say.

I don't need to fix . . .
There's nothing wrong with me.

> *There is if making me feel bad*
> *makes you feel better.*

He charges at me
when suddenly, a swarm of ladoos
from every direction fly

one
　　　　by
　　　　　　　　one
into his face.

I turn to see
Anju, Jasvinder, Zia, and even Varun
pelting the sweet balls,
and now I take my chance.

I block his punch and grab his shoulder

for Jasvinder

lift his head with the hook of my arm

for Anju

and flip him backward

for me.

Nirmal is f l a t
　　　　on
　　　　　　the

　　　ground,

while Anju, Jasvinder, and Zia,
along with the whole crowd,
who are cheering, count,

ONE . . . TWO . . . THREE!

KING

Cheers and whistles
explode along the
semicircle of gathered students.

Varun wraps his arms
around me.

*You were the only one
brave enough,* he whispers.

> *But you were strong enough
> to stand up for me,*
> I say, clasping his hand.

Then he raises an arm
in the air for silence.

*As our new King of the Field,
Raj will choose
the three new rules.*

All eyes watch
to see what I will do,
and all ears wait
to hear what rules I choose.

My eyes shine, imagining
a trail of kids behind me,
slapping me on the back,
doing whatever I say.

As it starts to drizzle,
my eyes catch sight
of the Indian flag,
the flag
that filled my nana
with so much pride
because its colors weren't just
saffron, white, and green,
but courage, faith, and peace.

Now his words swim
like the pallo
to the surface of my mind:
Being brave
doesn't mean you're not afraid.
It means
doing the right thing
anyway.

And I know what I have to do.

KINDNESS

Rule number 1:
> *No more King of the Field.*

A stirring of surprise
rolls through the crowd
as I walk toward the last place
they expect me to go.

Rule number 2:
> *No more gangs or tests.*

Mouths drop open
as I stand next to Nirmal,
who is holding his head,
squirming on the ground,
and offer him my hand.

Rule number 3:
> *Do the right thing,*
> *because our country needs*
> *less hatred and more peace.*

In the battering rain, I extend my hand,
not just to Nirmal,
but to Iqbal
    Uncle Bari, Tamir,
        Baba, Ammi, and Jana,
            the angry mob that chased me,
                the boy on the train,
                    and even the men with knives.

Nirmal hesitates,
then takes my hand.

        Why are you being so—

Because we don't need
your kind and my kind,
I say, helping him up,

only kindness.

GOOD FORTUNE

Everyone is silent,
as pearls spatter down from the sky,
and Anju claps,
then Jasvinder, Zia, and Varun follow,
and soon everyone
is cheering
      and dancing with relief
as my whole heart pulses
with happiness.

Come in out of the rain,
shouts Mr. Doshi,
rushing out of the school building,
waving frantically.

Nobody listens.

As the fresh, sweet drops
fall, steady and soft
from a sky of white velvet
with new life,
      cleansing,
           renewal,
               and always good fortune
we prance and soar off the ground
like rainbows,
and Sindh doesn't seem
so far away
after all.

BRAVE

I can't believe
you fought Nirmal! Anju says,
as we race home,
sailing over puddles
in the whooshing rain.

> *I can't believe*
> *I stood up to him!*

You stood up for me.
That was brave.

> My heart leaps.
> *You think I'm brave!*

Anju stops, dips her head.

That's the second time
you've saved me, Raj.

Suddenly, she's shy
when her large brown eyes
flick up . . .

> . . . and mine shoot down.
> I run my hand through my hair,
> wanting so much to tell her
> she's the one who saved me.
> That since she's come,
> > I sometimes forget
> > > that ache for home,
> > > > haven't felt alone,

but instead,
I shrug and say,
Anytime.

BLACK EYE

When Baba, Amma, and Vijay
see Anju's bruised chin
and my black eye,
they're furious.

What were you thinking,
getting into a fight at school?

Then Baba's kiss to my head
and tight embrace
tell me what his lips do not.
That he's with me,
truly forgives me,
and is filled with relief
that I am safe.

Later, when no one's watching,
Vijay drapes his arm
over my shoulder,
after Anju whispers
that Nirmal started the fight,
but I finished it.

Let me get this straight.
The guy picked a fight with you
and now he's your friend?

Vijay ruffles my hair
and shakes his head.

I'll have to mention that
in my next letter to Bhavna.

HEALING

I decide
to write to Nana again.

Talking to him
makes him feel closer,
and if I tell him
what it's really like here
    and tell him
    how I continue to miss him,
    maybe, just maybe,
        he'll write back
        to let me know
        he's still alive.

The one thing
I must tell him
is that I lost Maya.

It will break his heart
to know that she is missing,
but at least he'll know the truth,
and together we can pray
for her safe return.

It will heal my heart
to face my fear,
because even though I'm scared,
doing the right thing
sets me free.

DEAR NANA PART II,

I wasn't honest before.
I was scared when I wrote
to tell you about all the things we lost.
Now I know I need to do
the right thing anyway.

I'm sorry, Nana, but I failed
to watch Maya on the train
and she disappeared.
Since then, we have searched and I have prayed,
but we still haven't found her.

Baba, Amma, and Vijay
run a food business,
and they've earned enough money
so we can move out of Chacho Mohan's house,
which was feeling very crowded.

My favorite teacher at school is Miss Jhaveri,
and I made some friends:
Anju, Jasvinder, Zia, and Varun.
I even made a new friend today
called Nirmal.

Though I keep falling down,
I haven't forgotten your words to stand up
each time
and hold on tight
to the courage, faith, and peace
of the Indian flag,

which, like your words, continue to
guide me.

I still don't know
if I'll ever be as brave
as the silver pallo,
but I know that
Vijay's arm around my neck,
Baba's hand on my shoulder,
and Amma's kiss on my cheek
make my heart want to burst like a
ripe, sweet mango.

ALREADY

It is 132 days
since we've come to Bombay.

Vijay and I have found an apartment
on A-Road, in Churchgate,
says Baba.

It's not very big,
but it's close to a railway station,
a crescent-shaped promenade named Marine Drive,
that looks out to the Arabian Sea
and Chowpatty Beach.

Amma claps her hands,
Vijay squeezes me tight,
and my heart pounds as I tremble,
trying hard not to cry.

Though Marine Drive is not the Indus River
and Chowpatty Beach is not the Kirthar hills,
I can already see the colorful bobbing kites,
      smell the fresh, sweet-salty air,
           taste the pav bhaji masala food stalls,
                hear the rumbling of tumbling waves,
              and feel my suthan pants
                flapping in the breeze.

WRAPPED BUNDLE

We don't have much to take
other than our one case,
but Chacho Mohan insists
on driving us anyway.

Chachi Geeta embraces
each of us
and hands Amma
a wrapped bundle.

Just some saris and bangles
to replace what you lost.

Amma throws her arms
around Chachi Geeta,
who is only wearing
two of her gold bangles
on her wrists.

Asha and Beena cling to me,
asking if I'll come back soon
to play with them,
and I promise I will.

We're in the car,
meandering through congested streets
of hawkers, peddlers,
and potholes,
before we finally reach Churchgate.

After we say goodbye
to Chacho Mohan,

I take a deep breath
and follow the others
up four flights of stairs.

The apartment is bare,
    apart from
        a small wooden temple
        with mini Hindu god statues,
        Amma's agarbatti stand and bell,
            four thin mattresses
            on the floor of the bedroom,
                blinds as curtains,
                and a view from the window
                    of Marine Drive
                    and the rolling waves
                    of the Arabian Sea.

ALL WE NEED

Where is the furniture?
asks Amma.

> *We'll buy all that*
> *when we can afford it.*
> *For now, we have what we need,*
> says Baba, leading us to the kitchen.

On the polished counter
sits a matka for water,
round wooden chakla and belan
for rolling phulko and puris,
    a mesh charni
    for sifting atta flour,
    an aluminum tawa pan
    for roasting,
        a stainless steel kadai pot with deep insides
        for red gravy chicken and spicy pallo,
            a masala dabba with six tins for spices,
            a mortar and pestle
            for pummeling seasonings,
            a deep, small tadka pan
            for frying herbs,
            stainless-steel chimta tongs
            and a tea strainer,
                a jhara strainer for
                deep frying,
                and a vertical clay
                tandoor pot for
                baking meats.

Amma's eyes shine
as she takes in
all the brand-new tools
calling out to her,
as each of us
rolls up our sleeves.

WARM EMBRACE

It is 142 days
since we've come to Bombay,
a day before our visit
to the Kalyan Camp.

In our Churchgate apartment,
we gather around
the new dining table
that we bought with the money
from the orders
that Amma, Baba, and Vijay keep getting.
Amma stands up
and sways from side to side,
almost dancing to the music
only she can hear.

I'm happy to share . . . , she begins,
before her eyes water,
tears spill out,
and she turns away.

Baba goes to her,
places one hand under her chin,
and uses the other
to wipe her tears.

It's something
I've never seen
him do before.

Amma has used her hands
and heart
to save us all.
She didn't do it alone either,
he says, placing a hand on my shoulder.

His eyes are soft, meeting mine,
like a warm embrace.

You were right, Raj, to tell me
to let go and try something new.

Dado sutho. Very good.

KING OF HEARTS

Butterflies swirl
in the pit of my belly
as we stare into Amma's playful eyes,
and before she can speak,
the words
fly out of me.

You're opening a restaurant!

She smiles shyly
and nods.

We leap into the air,
spinning with excitement,
        and then debate
            where it will be,
                what it will be called.

While Baba and Vijay argue,
I whisper in Amma's ear,
Nana would be proud.

> *He'd be proud of you, Raj,*
> *and so happy to know that*
> *you found your strength.*

As King of the Kitchen?

> *As King of Hearts.*

KALYAN CAMP

It takes two hours
to reach the Kalyan Camp
in the car Baba borrows
from Chacho Mohan.

Everyone is still
bubbling with excitement
about the restaurant,
and I've never seen Amma
beam so wide.

We arrive at Section 2
of the camp's six sections
and are surrounded by
little boys hawking trinkets,
little girls selling strings of jasmine,
all wide-eyed,
with toothless grins
and rings of flies above them.

Quickly we move
through narrow barracks
and wider rooms,
where fifteen families
squash together,
shriveled old men, weary women,
small children barely clothed.

A boy in a tattered shirt,
so scrawny that his kneecaps
jut against his skin,
flutters wildly around us,

his dark hair like a rat's nest
and his eyes wild with curiosity
as he mutters to himself.

Cockroaches crawl
through piles of trash
as foul-smelling open drains
overflow with rats and mosquitoes.

In every room we pass, we ask
if anyone knows
the kind old lady that Anju calls
Aunty Padma.

They stare blankly and shrug,
each with the same reply:
Sorry, we do not know her.

After a three-hour search,
we give up.

> *I'm sorry we didn't find*
> *your aunty Padma,*
> says Amma, holding Anju's hand
> as we trudge back
> through the military barracks.

> *You look find Padma Didi?*
> asks the boy with the rat's-nest hair
> as he jumps and gestures
> and mumbles frantically
> for us to follow him
> before disappearing
> down a hallway.

GLIMPSES

We hurry after the boy
through large halls
the size of soccer fields,
which are subdivided into living rooms
smaller than Chacho Mohan's bathroom,
divided only by flapping gunnysacks.

We walk past a water tap
with a long queue of women
waiting to fill their plastic water pots.

We slip through rooms,
catching glimpses of
              a man complaining about bites and stings
              from field rats and snakes
                  and a group of people arguing
                  over their cooking oil and vitamin
                  tablet rations.

Then our wide-open eyes see
        a rugged man struggling
        to shave with no mirror,
                three silent women stitching cloth bags,
                  and a bald man sitting on the floor
                  marking papers.

This sea of sadness
threatens to drown
every survivor in this camp
who cannot swim.

SHARING

The boy, dizzy with excitement,
pulls back a blue sari screen,
revealing a woman sitting on a bed
with three children, two men,
and two other women.

When she sees us,
deep crevices fly wide across her face
and her eyes sparkle.

Oh, sweet Anju,
I knew I'd see you again!

> *Aunty Padma!* cries Anju,
> falling into the arms of a lady
> who is shrunken and pale,
> with wispy white hair.

The boy whispers in her ear
and she pinches his cheek.

Young Alok here
knows this camp
better than anyone.

> *We're so glad*
> *he helped us find you,* says Baba,
> giving Alok a four-anna coin.

Alok leaps and whoops,
bows and salutes us,
before rushing out of the room.

When we unpack our tiffins
filled with potato tikkis,
ridge gourd curry, chicken biryani,
mutton kofta, and koki,
Aunty claps her hands and licks her lips,
but Amma looks worried.

I didn't make enough.
How will we feed them all?
she whispers.

We can do it, Amma, I say.
We'll just give them one-eighth
of each of the five tiffins.

Amma reaches forward
to squeeze my shoulder.

You're doing it, Raj!
says Vijay.

Doing what?

Math,
says Baba
with a wink.

TURNING SILVER

When Aunty Padma
and her friends
have eaten their fill,
she pats her stomach.

This food is just so . . . so . . . ,
she starts to say
as tears form in the corners
of her eyes.

She stands to pray,
lighting her diya and incense sticks,
clutching her sandalwood beads
as she chants,
giving thanks for our visit.

As the agarbatti smoke
swirls from her puja thali plate
with a brass figurine of Krishna playing his flute,
she dips her finger in
blood red vermilion paste
and presses it
one
       by
              one
to our heads.

I see in the broken mirror
the red mark on my forehead,
like the red spot
on the silver pallo who is
brave, fierce, and strong enough

to survive
a hard journey,
sometimes even a storm.

SURPRISE

Dear Anju,
I have a surprise for you too,
says Aunty Padma.

Your doll, Devi—
I found her on the boat after you left
and kept her safe to give back to you.

> *You did?*

Yes, but then I met another little girl
who lost her family on the train,
so I gave it to her.

> *Oh,* says Anju.

I didn't think you'd mind,
because she reminded me
of you.

The five of us stare
    at one another
        all sharing the
            same thought
            same breath
                same wish
                    but each of us is
                        too scared
                            to speak.

What . . . was her name?
I ask.

Oh, she's gone now.
She left our camp with an older girl
to find her family.
But wherever she is, I'm sure Maya
is looking after your doll.

ALIVE

We are silent
for a whole minute.
Amma's eyes spill over
and tears slide down her cheeks.
    Then we laugh, cry,
        and soar like kites,
            throwing arms around each other,
              babbling
                and bursting
                  with questions.

Was she hungry?
    Was she scared?
        Where did she go?
            Will she come back?
                Are you sure her name was Maya?

Yes, says Aunty Padma,
and when she describes
the little girl
who drinks with a slurp,
wins card games, solves puzzles,
always grumbles of tummy pain,
and blinks her shiny eyes
to get whatever she wants,
Amma is sure
our Maya is alive.

HEALED

We say goodbye,
and I promise Aunty Padma
we'll come back soon
with food, clothes, blankets,
toys, and soap.

Thank you, Raj,
she says, taking my hands
and kissing my knuckles.
I stare down at them
and smile.

        We'll come often,
        very often, Amma says,
        as we walk back through the large halls.
        She takes my hand,
        as Anju clasps
        the other.

        Together.

HOME

On the walk back
to Chacho Mohan's car,
my steps are lighter
and I can feel the air in my heart
and lungs expand.

The sun blazes bright,
its rays bursting through
the raised Indian flag,
showering the campgrounds
with tinted hues
of saffron, white, and green.

Then Amma stops,
and we turn to see
the sun light up her face.

*I know the name
of our restaurant.*

She takes a deep breath.

Maya's Home.

DEAR RAJ,

Reading your letter filled me both
with the joy of watching a sky filled with stars
and a sorrow of knowing
that the bottom of a well
is empty.

    I was sorry to read about the nasty men
    and of everything you lost,
    but I am thankful that you are safe.
    You must now hold on tight
    and help the family build everything back.

        I, too, wish we could stroll together
        beside the Indus,
        but after you left, the violence spiraled,
        and one day, after cremating a woman's body,
        I was stabbed twice in the arm.

            My wounds became infected,
            and on my way to find a doctor,
            I collapsed on the street and would have died
            if it hadn't been for a kind young man
            whose family took me in.

                I lay in the young man's bed for weeks,
                fighting raging fever and hallucinations
                until one day, I woke up
                and had to look twice before smiling
                at my grandson's kite.

So I need to thank you, Raj,
for being as brave as the silver pallo
and bighearted enough to make peace
with Iqbal,
who, along with his baba and ammi,
saved your nana's life.

THREE COLORS

Three kites
rise up in long lines
on Chowpatty Beach,
cool salt breeze on our faces,
powdered sand between our toes.

Vijay's saffron kite teases, attempting
to cut down mine
as Anju's green kite dances,
pretending to jab at both of ours,
but none of us are using
a manjha.

As I look up
at our twirling kites
and wonder
what Nana and Iqbal are doing,
and when we'll finally
reunite with Maya,
I see that it no longer matters
how many days
it's been since we've come
to Bombay,
because even if there isn't
always a kite string to hold on to,
there's something else.

Hope.

AUTHOR'S NOTE

Partition forever changed the trajectory of my grandparents' and parents' lives—and therefore my life. As a little girl growing up in Hong Kong, when asked where I was from, I would repeat what my parents told me: "We come from a place in India that isn't in India anymore."

Years later, my daughter asked me a homework question: "Why do people migrate?" I told her our family was involved in the largest mass migration in world history. Though we now have a growing number of children's books about Partition, when we went to the library, we couldn't find one. My daughter accused me of making the whole thing up. It broke my heart.

In the years that followed, I read books, news articles, and testimonial archives and watched documentaries. I interviewed elders in the Sindhi community from around the world, many of whom spoke for the first time about their experience of upheaval and heartbreak.

India gained its independence from British rule on August 14–15, 1947. Soon after, British India was divided into India and Pakistan. Hindus and Sikhs were to live in India, and Muslims were to live in Pakistan, due to religious majority. Despite centuries of Hindus, Sikhs, and Muslims living peacefully alongside each other, this division forced underlying tensions between the different religious groups.

Partition led to history's largest and deadliest mass migration. Many had to suddenly leave, taking only what they could carry, giving up their homes and possessions and leaving behind neighbors and friends. It is estimated that more than fourteen million people were uprooted from their homes and at least a million people died.

Unlike the provinces of Punjab and Bengal, which were split in two, Sindh, where both my maternal and paternal grandparents lived, was given intact to the newly created nation of

Pakistan. Uprooted from their homeland and culture, Sindhi Hindus and Sikhs were forever displaced. Overnight they lost their homes, their community, and their sense of belonging.

The stories in this novel are their stories: the great-aunt who hid her neighbor's children under her sari; the young Hindu boy whose Muslim friend's topi saved his life; and my great-grandfather, Dada Lalchand Dhalamall, who chose to stay behind in Sindh to give a respectful cremation to the unclaimed bodies. He was never seen again.

To be faithful to the historical setting, I have included authentic Sindhi terms/spellings used by Bhaiband Sindhis of the time. One exception is the contemporary spelling of *Sindh* (spelled "Sind" prior to 1988) to help foster a sense of connection between young people around the world today and a cherished homeland reluctantly left behind.

Over time, our Sindhi language has been diluted and is slowly dying. And though the true essence of Sindhi meaning can never be fully captured when translated into English, I hope that this story of Sindh and its people, written in the most distilled language of verse, will be felt at its depth, as the poems stitch together in a way that heals and restores.

Though it was a time of great brutality, Partition also inspired moments of selfless compassion and humanity between Hindus, Sikhs, and Muslims. Many helped and protected one another, sometimes even at the risk of their own lives. There are stories of sacrifice, forgiveness, and lives rebuilt.

Tragically, the refugee crisis that resulted from Partition is not an isolated incident. Because of war, religion, the environment, or other factors, people continue to be displaced all over the world. From stories of the past, we can look beyond what divides us and see that we have more in common than we do differences. When we face loss and disappointment, we can remember that the only thing stronger than fear is hope.

Adhan: The Islamic call to public prayer in the mosque
agarbatti: Incense sticks
ajrak: A unique form of block printing found in Sindh
anna: A currency unit formerly used in British India, equal to one-sixteenth of a rupee
Ashoka Chakra: The blue wheel at the center of the Indian flag, representing life in movement
babul tree: A gum acacia tree native to Africa, the Middle East, and the Indian subcontinent
Bhaiband Sindhi: A Sindhi social grouping based on birth and kinship; members typically work as traders, shopkeepers, and businessmen
Bharat Mata ki Jai: A patriotic phrase meaning "Victory for Mother India" (Hindi)
canasta: A card game played with two packs, where the object is to score the most points by making melds in combinations of three or more cards, with a meld of seven being a canasta
carrom board: A tabletop game with a square board made of plywood and a pocket in each corner. Disks are struck by a striker, with the aim of pocketing the most disks, including the most valuable "queen" disk.
chaddar: A thin blanket
chador: A large piece of cloth wrapped around the head and upper body, leaving only one or two eyes exposed, worn especially by Muslim women
champals: Slipper sandals usually worn in the home
charpai: A wooden bedstead strung with tapes or light rope
chikoo: A rough, brown fuzzy-skinned fruit with sweet, juicy flesh. Also known as a sapodilla.
cholo: Traditional loose top worn by Hindu-Sindhi women
chor: Thief
dado sutho: Very good (Sindhi)

"Dama Dam Mast Qalandar": A spiritual Sufi devotional song, written in honor of the most revered Sufi saint of Sindh, Lal Shahbaz Qalandar of Sehwan Sharif (Punjabi/Urdu)

Diwali: The Hindu Festival of Lights

diya: A small cup-shaped oil lamp made of baked clay

dupatta: A long piece of cloth worn around the head, neck, or shoulders by women from South Asia

Eid al-Fitr: The Muslim holiday of breaking the fast

firangi: Foreigner (Hindi/Persian)

Gandhi, Mohandas Karamchand: The inspirational leader, peaceful activist, and legendary humanitarian, also known as the Mahatma (Great Soul), who helped India achieve independence

gilli danda: A game with four or more standing in a small circle, where a shorter stick (gilli) is hit by a longer one (danda). When the gilli is in the air, the player hits it as far as possible and runs to touch a pre-agreed point outside the circle before it is retrieved.

Hindustan Zindabad: A patriotic Hindustani phrase and battle cry (Hindi)

In shaa Allah: If Allah wills (Arabic)

jhoolo: A handcrafted wooden swing, also known as a peengho

Jhulelal: The most revered deity and river god of Sindhi Hindus

Jinnah, Muhammad Ali: The founder and first governor-general of Pakistan, revered as the father of Pakistan

juttas: Leather-made sandals (Sindhi)

kabaddi: A game with two teams of seven players, where a raider runs into the opposing team's half-court, touching as many defenders as possible and returning without being tackled by defenders and in a single breath

kaju mithai: A triangular Indian sweet made from cashew nuts, sugar, and ghee

kameez: A traditional long tunic top, usually paired with a shalwar

kara: A steel or cast-iron bangle worn by Sikhs

khadi: Hand-spun woven natural cloth promoted by Gandhi as self-sufficiency for the freedom struggle

Khuda hafiz: May God be your guardian (Persian/Arabic)

koti: A traditonal top worn by Muslim Sindhi women

kuro: Liar

kurta: A loose collarless shirt

ladoo: A spherical Indian sweet made from flour, sugar, and ghee

lathi: A stick used as a weapon, usually by the police or watchmen

limo pani: Lime water

lota: A round, handheld vessel for water

mangh: A triangular-structured wind catcher, almost like a chimney, typically fixed on housetops in Hyderabad and used to funnel in cool breezes

manjha: An abrasive string coated with glass powder used for cutting down kites

mehrbani: Please / thank you (Sindhi/Urdu)

mithai: Indian sweets usually made with flour, milk, sugar, nuts, and ghee

Moksha Patam: The original Snakes and Ladders, which was brought to the United Kingdom in the 1890s

muezzin: The person who calls members of the Muslim faith for prayer

mukhe maaf kajo: Forgive me, used when addressing an elder (Sindhi)

mukhe maaf kar: Forgive me, used when addressing someone your age or younger (Sindhi)

Muslim League: A political party founded in 1906 to safeguard the rights of Indian Muslims

namaz: Prayer

neh: No (Sindhi)

Nehru, Jawaharlal: The first prime minister of India in 1947, who worked with Gandhi to free India from British rule and was known as Pandit, which means "wise man"

ne kar: Don't do it (Sindhi)

pagri: A turban or headscarf worn by Sikh men. It is considered a great symbol of pride, identity, respect, and honor.

Pakko Qilo: One of the most prominent architectural landmarks of Hyderabad, Sindh

pallo: The most popular freshwater fish found in Sindhi cuisine, regarded as a gift from the Indus River. Also known as a hilsa or ilish fish.

papad: Black gram bean flour dough, either fried or cooked with dry heat (flipped over an open flame) until crunchy

paro: Traditional pants worn by Muslim-Sindhi women

patang: Kite (Hindi/Sindhi)

Patel, Sardar: Vallabhbhai Jhaverbhai Patel, who earned the title Sardar (leader), was known as the Iron Man of India for his contributions to the unification of the independent nation

patka: A head covering worn by Sikh children

phulko: Flatbread cooked on a tawa pan and placed on an open flame so it puffs up

puja thali: A round platter used for worshipping deities

Quaid-i-Azam: Great leader (Arabic)

Radcliffe Line: The borderline that separates India and Pakistan, named after Sir Cyril Radcliffe, a lawyer who, with no previous knowledge of or experience in cartography, determined the boundary line partitioning India and Pakistan within a period of five weeks

Ramadan: The ninth month of the Islamic calendar, observed by Muslims worldwide as a month of fasting

rummy: A card game where the object is to get rid of your cards by creating sets or runs

sambosa: A triangular pastry filled with spiced meat or vegetables

shalwar: Traditional baggy trousers, usually paired with a kameez

sherwani: An ankle-length, long-sleeved outer coat worn by men in South Asia

sheva: Selfless service (Sindhi); also spelled "seva"

Sindh: Prior to Partition, Sindh was a province of British India. Following Partition, with a Muslim majority of 70 percent, Sindh was given intact to the newly created nation of Pakistan. Sindh has a rich cultural and historical heritage and is home to the ancient Indus Valley Civilization, marked by two UNESCO-designated World Heritage Sites: the Makli Necropolis and Mohenjo-Daro.

Sindhi: A native of the province of Sindh and also the official language of Sindh

Sindhworki: Wealthy Hindu traders who spread their businesses overseas and typically traveled back home to see their families every two years

Singh, Bhagat: A charismatic revolutionary and renowned freedom fighter who became a martyr and folk hero after his execution at age twenty-three in 1931

Sufi: A believer of Sufism, with the spiritual goal of having a direct, personal experience of God

sujaag thi: Be alert (Sindhi)

suthan: Traditional pants worn by Hindu-Sindhi women

tirpun: A card game similar to whist for four players in partnerships of two, where the object is to make the most tricks by playing high cards in a suit or using a trump card

topi: A raised and rounded skullcap worn by Muslims. It is considered a great symbol of pride, piety, respect, and honor.

"Vande Mataram": A song that was a source of inspiration in the struggle for freedom, adopted as the national song of India in 1950. It translates to "I Praise Thee, Mother" (Bengali/Sanskrit).

vari garjandasi: We'll meet again (Sindhi)

ACKNOWLEDGMENTS

Mehrbani is one of the few Sindhi words I know, but it's a word I offer with great humility and a heart filled with gratitude to:

Rubin Pfeffer, my extraordinary agent—magical, brilliant, and a fierce champion for my work. Rubin, I can never thank you enough for your belief in this book and in me.

Amy Thrall Flynn, for believing in my words and my vision. I am so lucky to have your eyes, mind, heart, and relentless enthusiasm pushing my work ever forward.

Alessandra Balzer, my incredible editor, for seeing the potential in Raj's story and for loving these characters as much as I do. Your valuable insights, expertise, and keen editorial eye are unparalleled, and it is a privilege to work with you.

The team at HarperCollins / Balzer + Bray, especially Caitlin Johnson, Mikayla Lawrence, Emily Mannon, Patty Rosati, Mimi Rankin, Kerry Moynagh, Kathy Faber, and Jenny Sheridan. Valerie Shea, Veronica Ambrose, and Aisha Sabar for their careful reads. Cover artist Tara Anand and designer Celeste Knudson created the perfect cover for this book that is beautiful beyond my wildest dreams. So much happens behind the scenes to bring a book to life, and I am grateful to every one of you.

Rajani LaRocca and Maulik Pancholy, for dedicating your time and expertise in reading and crafting exceptional blurbs for my book.

Lesléa Newman, for changing the world one book at a time, and for changing my life through your wisdom, guidance, and friendship.

The SCBWI Hong Kong chapter, especially Mio Debnam, Rachel Ip, Laura Mannering, John Brennan, Sarah Rose, Stephanie Sy, Karla Sy, Michelle Fung, and Christina Matula, for your constant support of my work, with special thanks to Janet Mann for saying, "Oh, yes you can."

The TEDxTinHauWomen team, especially Treena Nairne, Karen Koh, and Stefanie Myers, for walking alongside me on my TEDx Talk journey, the seeds from which are planted in this book.

Saaz Aggarwal and Mohan Gehani, for your passion and knowledge of Sindh and for generously sharing your memories and the historical facts surrounding Partition.

Neha Tharani, Renu Tharani, and Sunita Khemlani, for helping me fact-check every term, cuisine, clothing, and custom representative of Bhaiband Sindhis in 1947.

Shikha S. Lamba, my bighearted friend, for pushing me to promote myself and my work, and for reading this book early and loving its pages.

Enormous thanks to all librarians, educators, and booksellers who help put books into the hands of young readers. Hometown hugs for my local independent bookstore, Bookazine, run by Shonee and Arti Mirchandani in Hong Kong.

To my huge, loving, incredible extended Sindhi community, especially my Hemnani, Dadlani, Melwani, and Mahtani families. Thank you for sharing your memories of heartache and hope. Thank you most for your tremendous encouragement and love. I hope that my words have done justice to the rich tapestry of our story.

Jaya Lalwani, my pillar and greatest cheerleader, along with Sonney, Deepa, and Karan, for offering your insights and endless support. Nameeta Dargani, for being right next to me in all things, even when you're all the way in Portugal. Jackie and Seema Surtani, for your level-ten enthusiasm in every step of my journey.

Ashok Hemnani, whose belief in me has pushed me to greater heights, and the late Meena Hemnani, who would have felt the thrill of holding this book in her hands at her very core. Mah, this was your dream too, and we did it.

Gope and Lavina (Meera) Melwani, for a childhood filled

with song, dance, and storytelling, and for your unconditional love, which has given me the deepest roots and strongest wings. Thank you for always believing in me. I am blessed to be your daughter.

Anoushka, Nadia, and Tarun Hemnani, for being my reason to strive and my motivation to be better. Know that you are loved beyond measure. Always dream big, chase those dreams relentlessly, and never be afraid to fail, for it is in failure that we find the courage to rise.

Sunil Hemnani, for making love, joy, and laughter the soundtrack of our lives. Master of the fairway, wizard of the kitchen, and hero of my heart—thank you for walking by my side, for holding my hand through the dark days, and for smiling widest when I fly.

Most of all, thank you, God. My rock, my refuge, and my truest confidant. Thank you for saving my life more than once and for working in my waiting.

To the survivors of Partition and anyone who has ever suffered unimaginable loss and had to start over again, I see you.

Lastly, to you, the reader: this book has come so far and finally found its way to you. Thank you for giving it a home. This story is yours now.